Marinated Money

A Helen and Frank Story

Marinated Money

A Helen and Frank Story

THOMAS MORGAN

TMH Books

ISBN: 978-1-7376747-2-6

Cover Design: Jodi Parrish

Dedication

To older people everywhere.

It was the best of times, it was the worst of times, it was the age of wisdom, it was the age of foolishness, it was the epoch of belief, it was the epoch of incredulity, it was the season of light, it was the season of darkness, it was the spring of hope, it was the winter of despair, we had everything before us, we had nothing before us, we were all going direct to heaven, we were all going direct the other way.

\- Charles Dickens, *A Tale of Two Cities*

Introduction

I planned the Helen and Frank series to chronicle the Covid-19 pandemic and the lives of several people in the Midwest who were trying to survive it. The first story began in September of 2020 when the initial Covid-19 lockdown eased, and people tried to return to a normal life. It ends in the spring of 2021. The couple met in a memory support center in St. Louis. After a rocky beginning, they fell in love, married, and encountered other existential problems. The second story, Marinated Money, takes Helen and Frank up to the end of 2021. Their involvement with organized criminals intensifies. The third story will continue their adventures into 2022 as the pandemic plays out. Readers will notice in these stories that some people dismiss Helen and Frank because they are old. Despite their age, they are wealthy and smart… and they are aggressive. These characteristics can get anyone into trouble.

By end of 2021 the pandemic of Covid-19 had dragged on for over two years. Millions of people had died. Economies had been disrupted; livelihoods shattered. Childhood development and education had regressed. Efforts to defeat the virus had largely failed. Vaccines had lessened hospitalization and death, but the advent of the Delta variant and then the Omicron variant in 2021 brought even more widespread infection. Politicians and their public health experts had made mistakes, the biggest of which was discounting natural immunity. Individuals who had recovered from Covid-19 retained long-lasting immunity against the virus. In mandating vaccination, natural immunity had been largely ignored, and people had lost their jobs for refusing vaccination. People argued constantly about who was allowed to make the rules. Natural immunity had turned the influenza pandemic of 1918 into an endemic disease within three years, but current authorities were slow to learn this lesson.

In the United States the fabric of civilization seemed to be fraying. Politicians had loosened the rules. Criminals were set free; borders were opened to illegal immigration, and law enforcement was marginalized. Shootings, assaults, robberies, murders, and suicides soared. Road and airline rage increased, and appalling rudeness became commonplace. Inflation raged. The resulting social disruption was blamed on everything but the obvious. People became angry and then grew despondent. They felt the ruling class had failed them.

Blood pressure and heart rate are easily measured. Stress is more difficult to assess, but it plays out in human behavior. People were stressed but did not recognize it. We seemed to be simultaneously living in revolutionary times and fighting a deadly virus. Americans were equally divided along political and social lines. The two factions selected different politicians and their experts to play the contemporary roles of Robespierre and Madame Defarge.

In this tumultuous upheaval Helen and Frank tried to live and prosper. They were fortunate that their wealth insulated them from the worst of these events. To escape urban chaos, they moved to the rural area of St. Albans, Missouri, just west of St. Louis. The move increased their isolation, but events continued to intrude. Their continued involvement with criminal elements did not help their situation.

- Thomas Morgan

Chapter 1

The late spring of 2021 brought relaxation of Covid-19 social restrictions in St. Louis. The mask mandate was dropped for fully vaccinated people, which meant it was effectively dropped for everyone. Social distancing was less strict, and more people were allowed into sports events, bars, and restaurants. However, some people found it difficult to give up their masks; indoor and outdoor events were marked by masked and unmasked people mingling and talking in close proximity. Helen Cohen Palermo and Frank Palermo gave up their masks but kept their distance from crowds. They continued to reside at the Big Muddy Hotel and Casino and to take most of their meals in their suite.

Three weeks after Helen had shot one hired killer and disarmed the other, Rex Raulerson, the manager of the hotel and casino complex, summoned Frank to his office.

"Thank you for coming, Mr. Palermo. How is your wife?" He asked, behind his mask when Frank took a seat.

Frank noticed Raulerson's mask was decorated with dollar signs and diamonds.

"She's fine. The whole thing was a shock to her, but she's doing well."

"I'm glad to hear that. It was a shocking incident. I hope you understand how much we are concerned for her."

"Yes, I appreciate that. I'll tell her about your concern." Frank figured Raulerson had more on his mind.

"What I wanted to say is that the shooting was difficult for all of us… for the hotel staff and all of our guests. The police have cleared her, I assume?"

Frank smiled at the rhetorical question. "Yes, they said it was self-defense and brought no charges about the unregistered gun although they confiscated it."

"I'm so glad to hear that. You know we don't allow firearms in the complex."

"It was your night desk guy who let the shooters into our suite."

"We have corrected that. He's no longer with us… but that's not what I wanted to talk about."

"What is it you wanted to talk about?" Frank had disliked Raulerson from previous meetings, and his distaste for the man was growing by the minute.

"Mr. Palermo, the long and short of it is that I'm afraid that you can no longer stay here. I'm sorry to say that, but we have to uphold our reputation."

"Your reputation?"

"Yes … we are a family-oriented establishment. We cater to that demographic."

"For the love of Pete, you run a freaking casino."

"Yes, but we are trying to cultivate a family atmosphere."

Frank laughed. "You've got prostitutes in the bars and parking lots."

"We are in the process of correcting that situation."

"So… let me be sure I understand this. You want us to move out because you think we are polluting your family atmosphere?"

"We would appreciate that."

Frank smiled at Raulerson's response and thanked him for his candor. Frank said he would talk to Helen about the matter. He rose and returned to his suite. When he entered, Helen said, "What was that all about?"

"They want us to move out."

"Why? What did he say?"

"He basically said it's because you're shooting people."

"Darling, those two were trying to kill us, and I only shot one of them. And he's likely to recover although he's going to have to learn to shoot with his other hand."

"I pointed that out to Raulerson, but it didn't seem to matter. I also think he's still mad about Charlie winning all that money at the tables."

"Maybe I should talk to him."

"Helen, my dear, I doubt that would help. He's mortally afraid of you already. I think we should find a house somewhere on the river and be done with these hotel people. Anyway, I'm tired of their cooking."

Helen considered the possibilities before agreeing with him. "Maybe you're right. We're too obvious here. We need a place with more security. By the way, I bought two new guns."

"I hope you registered them this time."

"Not yet, but I will. They'll be perfectly legal."

Frank wondered at Helen's continued disregard for the law and rules of polite society.

"I'll start looking for a place," he said. "You really must register your guns before something else happens."

"Good. I think somewhere south on the Mississippi or maybe on the Missouri overlooking the wine country. We're going to need some private security." Helen's faint smile indicated her distain for husbandly comments about her guns.

"I like the Missouri, out near St. Albans," Frank said.

"They already have security for some places out there. We could work with them. There's a high bluff I know about with beautiful views of the river and the valley. You can see all the way to the wine country."

Frank set about his assignment. He found a spacious house with a guesthouse on ample acreage above the small village of St. Albans — about 40 miles west of St. Louis. The house featured a panoramic view of the Missouri River as it wound its way south and east to join the Mississippi above St. Louis. He commissioned an agent to close on the house under an LLC he had created. Frank dreaded his notoriety brought on by the shooting. Keeping a low social profile had changed from a preferred lifestyle to a necessity for him.

When the sale closed, he established a security perimeter around the house with movement-sensitive infrared imaging, surveillance cameras, and silent alarms, and he signed a contract with a security company that served his gated community in St. Albans. Frank recognized that in the public eye he was a wealthy man. He needed a bodyguard with a physical presence, but also with the intelligence to run the technology that he had installed. In his mind that person was Barney Browning, the nursing aide at Beaumont. He knew Barney had worked in private security before taking the job at Beaumont during the financial meltdown in 2008.

When Frank offered him the job, Barney said, "Thank you, Mr. Palermo. You know I've been at Beaumont for over ten years. I'll have to think about it."

"So… it's *Mister* Palermo now," Frank said, a little taken aback. "What happened to plain old Frank?"

"The Frank I knew at Beaumont was a good man who was struggling with the loss of his wife. The Mr. Palermo I know now turns out to be a very wealthy man—wealthy beyond my imagination."

"Barney, I have confidence in your imagination. I'm offering you one hundred fifty thousand dollars, the guest house and a large expense account."

"Like I said, Mr. Palermo, I'll have to think about it. I'd also like to talk to Mrs. Palermo."

"Why Mrs. Palermo?"

"I'd be working for both of you. I'd like to hear her take on this."

&

Helen met Barney after she had finished her shift as a volunteer in Beaumont's dementia unit. She was seated at the conference table in the library when he entered. He took a seat at the other end, near the entrance. His size made the conference table look small.

"It's good to see you, Mrs. Palermo. The residents have missed you. We've all missed you."

"Thank you, Barney. You wanted to talk to me?"

"Mr. Palermo has offered me a job. I'm sure you know that. I want to be sure you agree with that idea."

"We talked about it. I'm fully on board. We bought a home out near St. Albans, and we need a security coordinator."

"What do you really know about me, Mrs. Palermo?"

Helen hesitated. She recognized that she was now being interviewed. "I know I like you. You've taken good care of us when we were at Beaumont.

I think you're competent and honest."

"Let me just tell you a few things about me. My family has been in this country a long time. We're descended from slaves who were brought over from Benin a long time ago. When my ancestors bought our freedom, which was long before the Civil War, we took the name Brown. It's a common name among people of color because we didn't want to use the name of our owners. In the late 19th Century, we changed our name to Browning, after the gun manufacturer. For people of color to legally change the family name wasn't easy in those days, but we did it."

Helen was uncertain where this conversation was going, but she decided to hear him out. "Thank you, Barney," she said. "I didn't know that."

"Let me tell you something about your family, Mrs. Palermo. You are descended from a family of New England shipbuilders and financiers. Your ancestors owned some of the ships that brought my ancestors to America."

Helen was temporarily at a loss for words. "I knew my mother's family came from New England, but I didn't know we were shipbuilders.

Barney, how do you know that?"

"We have to know things about people. It's how we have survived. In the old days we passed this information by letters and word of mouth. Now it's much easier with the internet."

Helen feared that Barney wouldn't take the job. "Where does that leave us, Barney?"

"I think it leaves us where we started. I wanted you to know something about me before I took the job. I like you and Frank. You're both good people, and I think that history from centuries ago should stay there and not always be dragged into the present."

"Thank you, Barney. I look forward to working with you. Do you mind if I tell Frank about our conversation?"

"I hope you do. I'm happy to move on from here with our present understanding."

Helen realized that Barney had seized permanent moral superiority with their brief conversation. "Can you tell me more about your family?" she asked.

"My family story will have to wait for another time. I have to get back to work. Thank you again for your time, Mrs. Palermo." With that Barney rose, signaling that the interview was over.

Helen marveled that what she had thought was a routine job interview had become a revelatory event for her. When she returned to her car, she phoned Frank and told him about the interview.

Frank laughed. "That sounds like Barney. He always knows things that surprise you, but don't underestimate him. He's the only staff member at Beaumont who knew all our faults and failings and still tried to help us."

"Why don't you forget the job and just give him some money? You've got plenty to spare. He makes me a little uneasy."

"He makes everybody a little uneasy. Part of that is his bulk. I make him about six feet eight and 300 pounds. But there's something else about him that's hard to describe. Even at half his size, he'd still be a formidable person. I can tell you one thing. When you need him, he'll be there for you."

Chapter 2

Helen and Frank's home was perched on a bluff on Wings Road in St. Albans, high above the curving Missouri River to the west and north. To the east, their view included the valley with the village of St. Albans and the golf and country club of the same name. It was an idyllic location with a panoramic view in every direction, but the best view was the Missouri River in late afternoon. The setting sun turned the winding river silver and gold, trimmed by verdant green in the spring and summer. Frank could imagine the river as a silver ribbon with white margins in winter. Barge traffic on the river looked like toy boats on a small stream. They both considered their terrace to have the best view in the entire state.

In another surprise, it turned out Barney had a wife, a strikingly beautiful woman named Moselle. They moved into the guest house quickly making it their own. Barney ran the surveillance and security operation adeptly, and Moselle found a managerial job at the golf and country club. Helen set up a firing range and a safe room in the sub-basement of their home. She installed enough sound proofing and a separate ventilation system around the firing range to isolate it from Frank's office two floors above. Frank spent every morning with his investment advisors, working remotely. Barney fine-tuned the security perimeter and scrubbed both houses of any surveillance devices. Helen calibrated her shooting skills.

The foursome often gathered on the terrace for wine and snacks at the end of each temperate day. Springtime was usually cool and wet in St. Louis, but the year 2021 brought some lovely days before summer's stifling heat and humidity set in. Charlie would sometimes join them for wine and conversation but being away from

Beaumont made him increasingly anxious and fretful. His short-term memory was clearly slipping away and with it went his emotional stability. Frank offered to get him a place at St. Albans with a housekeeper, but Charlie declined because he feared his time for independent living was growing short. He dreaded being on the locked dementia unit at Beaumont, but he saw no alternative in his future.

Frank routinely followed medical news as part of his daily search for investment opportunities. He checked out a newly approved treatment for Alzheimer's disease and found it would be several months before the drug was available, if at all. It would be expensive, but Frank did not care how much it cost if it would help Charlie. He was dismayed watching Charlie's mental decline.

Frank tried to join the country club and take up golf, but his reputation from the hotel shooting got him blackballed. Finally, several older members who remembered him from his restaurant days recommended him, and he was allowed to join with the caveat that Helen could not bring her guns into the club's buildings.

Helen said that restriction was acceptable. She could put her little Sig-Sauer in her bra holster, and no one would be the wiser unless they installed metal detectors and x-ray machines at the entrances. Moselle got credit for bringing in a new member, and Frank found golf to be much more difficult than it looked on television.

One beautiful evening in early June, Frank was sitting alone on the terrace, sipping a glass of Chianti Classico and listening to *la ci darem la mano* from Mozart's *Don Giovanni*. The mosquitos hadn't yet arrived. The air was warm and only mildly humid. Helen walked out and handed him his cell phone. "It's Vinnie," she said.

"Vinnie?"

"Vinnie, your nephew, in Chicago. He wants to talk to you." Helen's expression showed considerable doubt about Frank's memory.

Frank put the phone to his ear. "Hey, Vinnie, good to hear from you. How you doing?"

"Frank, I need to talk to you."

"This is a perfect time. I'm sitting here watching the lights come on across the river. What's happening?"

"Not on the phone, Frank. I need to come down there to talk to you."

Frank thought Vinnie sounded anxious and concerned. He couldn't remember ever hearing that tone of voice in his nephew. "Sure, Vinnie. Come on down. Stay a few days. We've got plenty of room."

"I need a secure place to talk… away from any listeners. Maybe out on the golf course or in that state park just down the road."

"Vinnie, this house is as secure as it gets. Barney and his team have scrubbed it clean. Come on down. We'd love to see you."

"Just you and me, Frank. This is family business. I'll be there tomorrow."

"How's Vinnie?" Helen said when he put down his phone.

"He didn't sound like the old Vinnie I know. He sounded detached and maybe a little afraid."

Vinnie appeared the next day at ten sharp in the morning, squired in a black Lincoln Coach Continental by a man in a dark suit. He dismissed his driver and walked up to greet Frank and Helen. They exchanged pleasantries, and Frank gave him a brief tour of the new abode. Helen opened a bottle of San Pellegrino, filled their glasses, and they sat down on the terrace.

Vinnie looked at Helen. "No offense, Helen, but this is a family thing. I need to talk to Frank alone."

"I hope you don't mind this too much, Vinnie, but Helen should stay. She's family now. She helped us both in our last brush with Tony Ragusa, and I've got a feeling your visit is about him."

Vinnie grimaced before he began his story. "It's definitely about Tony Rags. He's trying to take over my business, and I'm afraid he's got me in a tight place."

"I thought he was going to jail," Helen said.

"He's lawyered up pretty good. They're still wrangling about him moving money around and the gunfight at Beaumont."

Frank waited and Helen sipped her water.

Vinnie began again. "Back in the middle of the pandemic after you two got married and went to Florida, a bank and a group of investors came to me with a SPAC proposal. They wanted to merge and take my commercial real estate business public. They told me they had a bank that was fronting most of the money."

"SPAC?" Helen asked.

"That's short for special purpose acquisition company," Vinnie said. "It's a quick way to take a private business public. My real estate business had cratered during the peak of the pandemic, and I thought it was a good idea."

"What's their leverage, Vinnie?"

"I signed a memorandum of intent to go with them. Now they want to finish the deal and take me public."

"Is the document airtight? You might be able to wiggle out," Frank said.

"My lawyers are arguing with their lawyers, but the people in this SPAC can bring pressure you wouldn't encounter in a straight business deal."

"SPACs have fallen into disfavor," Frank said. "Many of them have failed to make any money—either they couldn't find a company to take public or couldn't find investors after they did."

"It's worse than a straight up SPAC anyway. Turns out the bank and its backers were fronting for Tony and some of his so-called investors. I guess they figure they can beat me on the financial angle now. With the commercial real estate business still down after the pandemic, they're pressing to buy me out at pennies on the dollar when they take over. That way they can screw me now and get the chance to screw the public later."

"How much are they into you for?" Frank asked.

"About a round billion if you figure what my business is worth when things really open up again. They'll wipe me out with this deal."

"The whole thing sounds way too sophisticated for Tony."

"Tony is changing his operation," Vinnie said. "He's hired some MBAs from Wharton, and he's bent them to his nefarious ways. He's getting into more subtle and lucrative forms of fraud. Street operations with drugs, gambling, extortion, and shakedowns have become too dangerous, even for Tony's crowd. Tony had to change because Chicago has changed."

Frank whistled softly; Helen sipped more water. "I can help with the money," Frank said. "But they'll still walk away with a big profit even if they can't sell many shares."

"You have that kind of money?" Vinnie was clearly surprised.

"Yes, I do, but it will pretty much tap me dry."

"Why don't we turn the tables on them? I think I know how to do that." Helen said.

Both men stared at her, slack jawed. They knew that when Helen hatched a scheme, strange things could happen.

Frank tried to gather his wits. "If it's a SPAC and a total default swap behind it, the bank is the one carrying the risk. We need to know more about the bank in this deal."

Vinny was astonished. "How do you know all this, Frank? You sound like my accountants."

"Vinnie, I've spent every morning for the last five years trying to learn everything I can about finance and investments. It was how I kept myself sane … until Helen came into my life. She has greatly helped with my sanity too."

Helen remained silent, sipping her water. Vinnie mentioned the name, Sunshine Investment Bank; Frank picked up his landline to make a call.

"Wait!" Vinnie said, "We have to be sure nobody's listening."

"Vinnie, if this line's not secure, we'll have to go back to using pigeons. I know a forensic accountant who used to work at my bank, and she's the one to follow the money in this deal."

Frank called and talked to the accountant, Rachel Bruggemann, on speaker phone. She agreed to look into the matter and asked for information from Vinnie about the SPAC proposal. Vinnie said he had to get back to Chicago, but that he would have a man deliver the documents to her office tomorrow. She replied that she had a secure fax line, and Vinnie said there's no such thing as a secure line.

Helen and Frank convinced him to stay for lunch, and then saw him off in the black Lincoln with the swarthy, black-suited driver.

As the car departed, Frank looked at Helen. "Vinnie says he runs a legitimate business, but he certainly tries hard to look like a gangster."

"I know he's family, and you two go back a long way," Helen replied. "But I wouldn't give him the kind of money you're talking about. I don't think you'll get it back."

"He'll give it back if he can. I remember he gave my money back after I covered what you and Jamie stole with your software scam."

"Darling, let's don't go digging up the past. I'm genuinely sorry about that episode. You will remember that I helped get it back, won't you?"

"I don't forget things like that, my dear. Anyway, we have more money than I told him."

"We do? Perhaps we both should meet with your bankers. If you were to get hit by a bus, I wouldn't know where to start."

"We can certainly set up a meeting if you like, but all you have to remember is to look in our safety deposit box. There are detailed instructions in there. Take the instructions to any vice president in the private bank department, and the process will be like a walk in the park."

"You're making this too easy. How do you know I won't shoot *you* for your money?"

"First of all, my dear, your religion prohibits it, but your past performance also argues that you won't do it. If you didn't kill the hired assassins when you had the chance, you're unlikely to try to kill me."

"I had to shoot him in the arm. He was wearing body armor."

"Anyway, we've got enough money for both of us. And we're new rich. Our money needs to be enjoyed right now."

"As a good Catholic, don't you ever worry about being rich … feel guilty about it? Didn't Jesus say, 'money is the root of all evil'? I think I remember that."

"Actually, it was the Apostle Paul. He said something like 'the love of money is the root of all evil.' I think he was talking about where your mind is, not your money."

"How do you know all this stuff?"

"Between my mother and the good Sisters in school, I got a thorough grounding in Holy Writ and the catechism. It was enough to last me a lifetime. Let me remind you that money is also a prime topic in Jewish scripture. We have been doing the wrong things with wealth since people figured out how to get rich. And that was a long time ago."

"I'll have to take your word for that."

"My point is there are some families in St. Louis with wealth that goes back two hundred years or more. Angie used to say they had marinated money. Our money is new and needs to be enjoyed now."

"Oh, marinated money, I love that! St. Louis has always struck me as a peculiar place — friendly but also very reserved."

"It's definitely that. Now don't get me wrong; I dearly love St. Louis, but the city is so old it's developed its own particular class structure. The Spanish and French came first and pushed the native tribes out to the west. Then with the Louisiana Purchase it became American on paper. After that, new immigrants came in from Germany and Italy. More immigrants from all over the world followed them. What you see across the river from our house is mostly vineyards started by Germans well over a century ago. With all the different immigration came the class divisions."

"Where do you fit in?"

"I'm easy to peg — a second generation Sicilian, and barely a high school graduate to boot. That's pretty low on the pecking order. In this town, the Protestants aren't sure about the Catholics, and the old money resents the new money. Plus, the different parts of the country all run together here. I think we tend to favor the East and the South. Kansas City looks more to the North and the West."

"The Blacks don't seem to be doing very well."

"That's true in the city. Black people who have moved to the suburbs have improved their lives, but many young Black men in the city seem to be on a path to destruction. There are gunfights in the city every night. If they survive to age thirty, they have a chance, but they're still held back by a poor education and limited economic opportunities. It all makes me sad. People are afraid to go downtown."

"What about the Jews?"

"They've done pretty well in St. Louis as they have in many other places. They've gotten themselves educated, and many of them have made money."

"But you've got money."

"Yeah, but it's not the right kind of money; it's new money--not money and prestige passed down for generations. In this town that's what counts — but it often comes with a disadvantage that's hard to shake."

"What's that?'

"The old money people tend to be insular. The go to the same schools, join the same clubs and go into business together. They tend to marry within their circle, and their children repeat the same cycle. They miss opportunities because they're locked into a certain way of thinking. Now please hear me on this. That's a problem with old money anywhere you go. There's much to like about St. Louis. We celebrate our traditions and heritage, and we tend to help each other out. We've pretty much always welcomed immigrants."

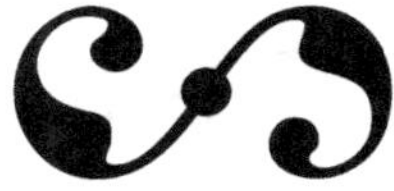

Chapter 3

Frank had liked Rachel Bruggemann from the first time she steered him away from a bad investment, and his admiration for her grew the more they worked together. Rachel could not only identify a misleading financial report; she had the uncanny ability to smell the taint behind it. She could get into the structure of the organization making the report and into the minds of those who had prepared it. Frank suspected that she had some advanced hacking skills, but he never intimated this to anyone. He didn't want to know Rachel's methods; he was only interested in her results.

After several days, she arranged a video conference with Frank and Vinnie. Helen joined them at her request; Vinnie did not object.

"First of all," Rachel said, "let me thank you both for this opportunity. I've always enjoyed working with Frank, and now I'm delighted to get to work with the younger Mr. Palermo. It's also a pleasure to meet you, Mrs. Palermo."

"I've underestimated Uncle Frank too many times lately," Vinnie said. "I'll try not to do that again. Thank you for helping us."

Rachel smiled and laid out her findings. "Sunshine Investment Bank is chartered in both the United States and the Bahamas. It was set up as a development bank in 2019 to aid the Bahamas after Hurricane Dorian. Then organized crime quietly took it later that year."

"So … it's a foreign bank," Frank said.

"Not exactly. It holds a dual charter, but they operate it in a way that makes it look like a Bahamian bank. The bank's owners have links to organized crime, and all the deposits and securities are held in Nassau with a storefront in West Palm Beach. They've given a little money to rebuilding the northern Bahamas after the hurricane, but that's only been a token to keep their dual charter. The bank's assets have grown very large with South American drug profits."

"What's the risk for the bank in my SPAC deal?" Vinnie asked.

"They've structured it as a total default swap… like a family wealth fund might do with a bank. Mr. Ragusa is putting up fifteen percent of the money, and Sunshine is putting in eighty-five percent. That's pretty easy for the bank since the principals own a large portion of the bank's deposits. They must be expecting a big payoff."

"What's the total amount they've raised for my deal?"

"It's about five hundred million U.S. dollars."

"I knew it! They're planning to pick up my business on the cheap. Then they'll sell shares and make a pile of money. Hell, they'll make money just taking over my business. They'd be getting it at a huge discount."

"If it plays out the way they intend, you're right. But Sunshine is taking a big risk in this deal. The bank stands to lose a lot of money if their plans don't work out. You will remember some recent large family wealth funds essentially disappeared when they concentrated their investments on a small number of volatile securities in these bank swaps, and in the process, they tarnished the images and balance sheets of several big banks."

"How could we screw them?" Vinnie asked.

Rachel was clearly taken aback. "I would guess the easiest way to thwart them would be to have another investor enter the picture and offer to buy your business at a premium. They would either have to back away or get into a bidding process."

"I mean really screw them."

Rachel frowned at Vinnie's language. "I suppose you could take their money and then buy all the shares when they go public, but that might not be the best solution."

"Vinnie, please remember who we're dealing with here," Frank said.

"I don't care. I've done very well, running a legitimate business with no help from these guys, and now they're trying to steal it."

"Rachel, what do you think is the best solution?" Frank asked.

"Let me start with a little background. A memorandum of intent is a halfway document. It helps the signers to move to a completed contract, but it is not absolutely binding. Your lawyers will know the ins and outs of this better than I do. I suggest you continue to have the lawyers wrangle about the legality of the paper you signed, and in the meantime, find a prospective buyer with deeper pockets to increase the pressure on them and their bank."

Helen finally spoke. "I can recommend a buyer with very deep pockets. That would flush them out."

"My pockets are pretty deep," Frank said. "I have enough to call their bluff."

"Darling, I'm delighted to know you have deep pockets, but we also need someone with a big scary reputation for acquisitions. Someone scary enough to throw them off their game."

"Given the right circumstances, my dear, I can be scary when I need to be."

They ended the videoconference on that note—Helen feeling ignored and Frank trying to be scary. Events over the next few days did not improve their domestic situation. Life in the countryside saw to that. Helen complained that the deer and rabbits were eating her flowers and vegetables, and Frank grew tired of his own cooking. Finally, he suggested Helen get a dog to scare the deer and rabbits. Helen countered that Frank should hire a food service. Helen said she had never had a dog and doubted she could train it. Frank was chagrined that his culinary interests were declining. They left both domestic decisions hanging for several days during which Helen spent more of her time at the country club talking to Moselle and helping with membership recruitment. Helen's frequent presence at the club didn't sit well with some of the members because of her history of shooting people, but her skill in bringing in new members quieted their misgivings. Helen had gained considerable notoriety, and prospective members wanted to meet her and talk to her.

She returned home from the club late one afternoon and said, "Have you seen Barney's office? Moselle walked me through there this afternoon. It looks like mission control for a NASA operation."

"I haven't seen it," Frank said. "But I want to talk to you. I think the way we're behaving is crazy. Here we've been married less than a year, and we're fighting over something I don't understand. You're clearly unhappy and that makes me unhappy."

"Let me explain it then. I'm feeling ignored. You're treating me like a dumb blonde. I'm not as smart as you are with money, but I have more street smarts than you do. I think I know how to throw Tony and his boys off their game."

"Alright, I'm listening."

"Well, there are some people in Omaha with very deep pockets. If we make Tony think they're interested in Vinnie's business, it could scare him off or start a bidding war."

"You're talking about ...War?"

Helen abruptly interrupted. "Don't say his name! Tony can figure it out, and we can avoid any liability if our plan goes public. Here's what we should do." With that Helen launched into a detailed description of the financial trap she intended to lay and bait. Frank marveled at her ingenuity and at the same time recognized that she might have a good idea.

૭

When Frank visited Barney's office the next day, he was surprised to see three walls of computer monitors around a central console with several tablets and keyboards. "What's up with all the hardware, Barney? You don't need all this for our security system."

"Frank, I told Mrs. Palermo that my family originally came from Benin ... in Africa. Did she tell you?"

"She mentioned something about it," Frank lied. He had never heard of Benin.

"Well, a long time ago ... at about the end of the 19th Century the British went in there and settled a trade dispute by machine-gunning a bunch of my people and looting the king's palace. They stole the Benin Bronzes from King Oba and the Edo people."

"I've heard of the Benin Bronzes," Frank's memory awakened.

"In those days the Brits were good at that... stealing from people they thought were their inferiors. It was kind of their version of *Droit du Seigneur* when they built their empire."

"What does that have to do with you, Barney?"

"It has everything to do with me. We mean to get those bronzes back. I'm one of the coordinators in North America for restitution of the bronzes."

"Barney, you're obviously a few steps ahead of me. What are you actually trying to do?"

"It's a long story, Frank. The Brits stole them from us and then sold them to museums and private collectors around the world. Now the self-appointed experts are saying the museums and collectors should keep them because only they can protect and preserve the bronzes. The poor Africans in Nigeria wouldn't know how to do this. The arrogance and condescension of these so-called experts amazes me."

"Please tell me more."

"A group of wealthy Africans and Blacks here in the states have organized to get them back. The bronzes in the U.S. are in several museums or held by private collectors. Right now, we're buying out the private collectors and trying to shame the museums."

"Barney, I'm not judging you, but let me remind you that we're paying you to be our security coordinator."

"I'm doing this at night. I also monitor the surveillance systems at the same time. And all this extra hardware comes from the African consortium. I'm not spending your money."

"What's in it for you? Why are you doing this?"

"I'm doing it because the British stole the bronzes from us, and now the world wants to keep them. The experts are saying they should keep them because we don't have the intelligence or facilities to preserve and display them. That's pure bullshit! We are currently building a museum in Lagos for that very purpose. And there's another museum in Lagos that already has some bronzes. All the Benin Bronzes will be where they started and where they belong."

Frank felt like a bystander in a drive-by shooting, but he kept his silence because to Barney the matter was clearly serious.

"Alright, Barney. I don't have a horse in this race, but I'll support you. Just remember you're going up against a lot of entrenched money and influence."

"We know that, but we figure we can get them on the racial angle. They're mostly white and we're all Black. The ones we can't shame, we'll buy out at low dollar. You get on the web right now; you'll see people trying to sell their Benin Bronzes. Of course, most of what they're selling is fake, but we're buying back the good pieces."

"Good luck."

"Thanks, Frank. I won't let this interfere with my real job."

When Frank walked back to his house he was greeted by barking. Opening the door, he was nearly toppled by a small bundle of fur and bulk. Helen had brought home an Australian Shepherd puppy. The pup's present appearance and strength promised a formidable animal upon reaching maturity.

"I was thinking you'd get something with more bark than brawn. This dog is going to get large."

"That's the idea," Helen said. "This breed can back up their bark. And they're fantastically loyal. We're going to love this little guy."

"What are you going to name him?"

"I don't know yet. I want to see how he develops. How do you say big dog in Italian?"

"*Grande cane* is one way. Is this dog a boy or a girl?"

"I'm not sure. Anyway, pretty soon this dog will be neutered. Then it will be an 'it.' Let's try Cane for starts. Do you think you can teach him Italian?"

"It'll probably just confuse him. One language is enough for a dog. Hell, it's more than enough for most people. I guess now I'll have to get a food service."

"Just try it, darling. If you can find one you like, it will take a load off your shoulders and give you more time to rest. Then you can cook only when you want to. I'm sorry I'm not a very good cook."

"You have other qualities that make up for any lack of culinary skills."

Chapter 4

Tony Ragusa took the largest chair in his conference room in Chicago for his weekly staff meeting. His assistants ran through the financial reports on his waste disposal business and then presented results from his loan sharking, extortion, healthcare fraud, and federal CARES Act fraud operations. Tony was pleased with their PowerPoint presentation until they got to the SPAC takeover of Vinnie Palermo's commercial real estate business. Progress there had come to a halt.

"What's the problem?" Tony said.

"Their lawyers are making it hard for us in general. This week they've hinted they have another buyer for Mr. Palermo's business." An assistant said.

"Who? Who wants to buy his business?"

"It's not clear yet, but we think it's his uncle, Frank Palermo."

"Old Frank? He doesn't have enough money to buy a food truck."

"Actually, sir, we think he does. As best we can tell he's got over fifty million U.S. dollars of liquidity."

Tony was stunned. "You kidding me? I can't believe it. Old Frank the really rich guy, and Annie Oakley, his gun-toting wife. I'll bet she figures in this somehow. What a pair—both of them escaped from a nursing home for the mentally retarded. This is rich!"

The assistant smiled at the unintended pun. "I believe it was a memory support unit, sir. We'll continue to investigate, of course, but I think they have a strong case to ignore our memorandum of intent."

"Old Frank may have the money, but he doesn't have the *cujones* for this kind of work. Tell Vinnie's people we're moving forward on the SPAC, and you can raise our offer to two hundred million for his buyout."

"We should probably check this out with our bank," his consigliere said.

"Just do it. You guys worry too much about the small stuff. If old Frank doesn't cave, we'll just have to put some muscle on him."

The assembled assistants stood and gathered their papers and laptops. "And light a fire under our hackers," Tony said to their backs. "We need to get deeper into old Frank's accounts and files. What am I paying these guys for anyway? I don't believe much of what they've been getting on him so far." He smirked and lit a cigar.

❧

When Frank and Barney met for their weekly review two days later, Barney said, "We're being probed from all directions. They are trying to penetrate our security through the front door, side doors and back door."

"You think the attack is coming from Ragusa?"

"Probably, but our security people say there's some Eastern Europe fingerprints on it too."

"Sounds like Tony has gone international. Keep leaking the default files to them. And let them know that Vinnie's flying to Omaha to meet with a prospective buyer. Leak it as an email from Vinnie to me. Make sure you give dates and times so Tony can check it out."

Vinnie's plane landed at Omaha's Eppley Airfield at dusk on a Friday in late July. He and two assistants exited the plane after dark and were driven to the Omaha Marriott Downtown where they stayed until midday on Sunday. People in suits with laptops and briefcases were seen streaming in and out of Vinnie's suite on a regular basis. He did not leave the hotel except to dine in a private room at Gorat's Steakhouse on Saturday night. When he departed on Sunday, he made sure that he and his assistants were in full view.

Tony monitored the visit as it happened by placing men at the airport, in the downtown hotel, and at the steakhouse. His men made detailed notes and took video of the entire weekend, but they gained little information. When they returned to Chicago, they assembled for a debriefing with Tony and his financial advisors.

"Vinnie didn't go to Omaha for a vacation," said Tony. "He must be meeting with that Buffett guy. How come you boys didn't get him on video?"

"We carefully monitored the suite's visitors and the restaurant. We never saw Mr. Buffett or Mr. Munger or any of their top associates meet with Mr. Palermo."

"You checked with his investment outfit?"

"Berkshire is very quiet about upcoming investments. They basically gave us a 'no comment' on all our questions."

"Well, I'm thinking Buffett is the mystery buyer. He's into real estate. It figures he would be interested in Vinnie's business."

"Actually, sir, he's been investing more in residential real estate, and he's franchising that effort. Commercial real estate would be a new direction for him."

"It's all real estate. Buffett's sitting on a pile of cash. And he's not a wild guy; he's cautious. He'll probably back out if we start a bidding war."

"It's more like a mountain of cash, sir. He's got over one hundred billion U.S. dollars available right now."

"That's what I'm saying. Vinnie's business is chump change for him, but it's a door into commercial real estate. If he thinks he's buying it cheap, we're going to make him pay for it. I also think it's time to put a scare into old Frank." Tony chortled and lit a cigar.

"Now get our hackers back to work on Vinnie and old Frank," he said. "And financial people keep pushing up our offer… but a little bit at a time. I want them to know we're serious but not stupid rich. We'll see if they're got the stomach for what we're doing."

The last half of July brought a new wrinkle in the Covid-19 pandemic. A virus mutation called the delta variant proved to be especially contagious and was spreading rapidly. It wasn't particularly lethal and only caused a small increase in deaths, but more people became ill enough to require hospitalization. The media pumped this latest development as if all previous measures against the virus had failed, but the delta variant was mainly infecting the unvaccinated. The vaccines had been proven to be effective repeatedly, but about one-third of adults still refused vaccination. Political and health authorities began pushing for indoor masks again—even in vaccinated people. Fears returned of schools not reopening and the imposition of another lockdown. Lawsuits proliferated about the new mask mandates, and some politicians issued edicts banning mask mandates. Major employers and some colleges began to insist on vaccinations.

Commercial real estate remained depressed because people wanted to work at home. In St. Louis County, the county executive ordered the return of masks in indoor public gatherings. The elected county council voted to cancel the order, and the state attorney general sued the county to overturn the new mask mandate. All these developments left people confused. It became common to see masked and unmasked people mingling in supermarkets, restaurants, and other public venues.

The surge of the delta variant put extra stress on Vinnie's business. Several of his large construction loans were coming due, pushing him closer to completing the SPAC deal. In video conferences with Frank and his financial people, Vinnie had nearly decided to go forward with the SPAC deal, but then Tony raised the stakes as only he could do. It happened late on a Sunday night in early August when Barney detected movement in the woods leading up to their enclave above St. Albans.

"Frank, we've got movement in the woods below us," Barney reported with a text to Frank's cell phone.

"Probably just some deer out there," Frank texted back.

"I don't think so. Our trail cameras are seeing human forms. Looks like two adults." Barney had switched to a cell phone call.

"Let's check them out."

"Negatory, boss. Please don't try to be a hero. That's what you're paying me for. You and Helen go to the safe room. I'll take care of these two."

Frank reluctantly complied. He woke Helen, and they and their puppy hurried to their safe room in the sub-basement. Barney put on dark camouflage clothing and night vision glasses and silently descended to a small coppice of trees and brush in the direct path of the approaching intruders. He crouched in the brush as the two men walked past, dressed in black and wearing night vision glasses. Each carried a package that looked like an incendiary device. Barney rose and silently followed them. When they paused, he stepped up and cracked their heads together with his massive hands. Their only sound was a muffled groan as they went down.

Barney checked for breathing and pulse. They were unconscious but very much alive. He quickly stripped them of shoes and outer clothing. They carried no identification, but each had a cigarette lighter, and one had a key fob for a vehicle. As he suspected, the packages were thermite devices with a common sparkler sticking halfway out. It was an easy device to make and was legal as long as it wasn't used for a malign purpose. Barney guessed their plan was to destroy the air conditioning in the main house. Without air conditioning, the house would be extremely uncomfortable in August. They had done their homework because they obviously knew there were two outside AC units in the main house. Barney figured they had been using drones for surveillance. He smiled and shook his head. These thugs gave new meaning to the term turning up the heat. He stuffed their clothing and shoes into his backpack. He also took the key fob, cigarette lighters and the incendiary devices, leaving the thugs in their underwear and socks, breathing heavily. They would have some explaining to do when they walked into the village of St. Albans in the morning.

Barney took out his cell phone as he walked back to his house. "I took care of them, Frank. I think they were trying to burn up your AC."

"Please tell me you didn't kill them."

"No, of course not. But they're going to have headaches in the morning. I don't know who sent them, but I'll give you one guess. They had no ID. Tonight takes me back to my special ops days."

The thugs had been smart enough to hide another key fob near their vehicle at the foot of the bluff. When they regained consciousness shortly before dawn, they staggered down to their vehicle. They retrieved the key fob and found their handguns under the front seat. They briefly considered going back up the hill for a shootout to salve their wounded pride, but the thought of doing it in their underwear and socks dissuaded them. They drove back to their airport hotel just after sunrise. On their way, they stopped at a Wal-Mart Superstore and bought pants, shirts, and shoes. After showering they began formulating their report to Tony.

While Tony's two failed arsonists tried to regroup, Frank, Vinnie, Barney, and Rachel met by video conference. Barney detailed the cybersecurity threat and described his adventure in the night with the two would-be arsonists.

"That just about does it from our end!" Frank said. "I don't know about you, Vinnie, but I've had it with them… coming down here trying to burn me out breaks the deal."

"I agree," Vinnie said. "I'm not cooperating with Tony on this or any other deal. The little rat can't be trusted. Let's bid up this SPAC deal with them. I want to screw them now more than ever."

Back in Chicago later that day Tony listened to the phone report from his two nocturnal operatives in St. Louis. They gave him a carefully edited version of their activities in St. Albans, but Tony was no fool. He told them to fly back to Chicago and submit a verbal report. He glared at his advisors as he put down his cell phone. "What the hell is going on?" he said. "I send those two *cazzoni* down there to give old Frank a scare, and now they want more money for a job they didn't do? Will somebody please do something right around here?"

"They needed to buy some clothing. They're saying that replacing their clothing wasn't part of the contract and they want to be reimbursed," said an assistant who had taken a preliminary call from the hapless duo.

"The hell they say! They lose their pants down there, that's their problem. I keep sending *idioti* to do a simple job, and they keep screwing up. Do I have to go down there myself and deal with old Frank and Annie Oakley? This thing is taking way too much of my time. And it's making me very mad. Now, get my financial people in here. I want to close on this SPAC. I'm getting very tired of anybody with the name of Palermo."

Chapter 5

In this way, negotiations proceeded on the SPAC-funded buyout of Vinnie's business. Tony was determined to merge with Vinnie's operation and take it public, which would give him a large piece of the commercial real estate business in Chicago and then to sell shares to an unsuspecting public. Vinnie was equally determined to make Tony pay a prodigious price for that privilege. On several occasions Tony thought he had a deal, and then Vinnie's people would back away and say Vinnie had a better offer from another interested party. By the end of August, Tony had exhausted his patience, which was never a prominent virtue for him.

"What are you guys doing about the SPAC?" he asked at his weekly staff meeting in late August.

"We think we have a deal, sir," his consigliere replied.

"What's the bottom line for me?"

"Mr. Palermo's buyout is up to about two hundred million, which would put your obligation at about thirty million."

"You checked this number with our bank?"

"Well… not exactly this specific number. They gave us authorization to go up to five hundred million on their end."

"You boys think Vinnie's really going to sign off on this?"

"He's giving us every indication we are the winning bidder at this point."

Tony smirked. "So … I backed old Buffett down on this deal. I knew I could do it. We get our hands on that real estate business, we're going to be knee-deep in money."

His consigliere thought they'd more likely be knee-deep in manure, but he said, "Congratulations, sir. Mr. Palermo is expected to sign off on the buyout later this week. In the meantime, we'll get all the paperwork together to close the SPAC and usher Mr. Palermo out of the real estate business."

❧

Helen and Frank were sitting comfortably in their living room with a view of the Missouri River far below them. It was near dusk in late August. The sun was setting earlier now, but the days remained hot and humid. Their terrace was uncomfortable, especially in late afternoon. Luckily, their great room offered them a similar panorama. The setting sun cast shadows through the green vineyards beyond the silver reflection of the river. A medley of Puccini arias played softly as they sipped a vino Veneto and commented on the craziness of the world. Neither Helen nor Frank was particularly political, but Covid-19 and the social unrest that attended the pandemic seemed to always bring their conversations back to the political. They didn't think politicians were making good decisions around the world, and the situation was frustrating because they didn't have better solutions to offer.

The Covid-19 pandemic had now dragged on for eighteen months. Vaccines seemed to be losing their protection over time, with increasing breakthrough infections by the delta variant happening. There was general talk of booster shots in the fall. People were tired of the virus and the death and misery it had caused. People also felt an unfocused anger and general frustration, which played out with increased incidents of road rage and inflight airline passenger aggression. Many people seemed to distrust their government and health officials. Helen heard it at the country club, and Frank heard it every morning in his remote financial meetings. It was as if the public had disaster-fatigue—the debacle in Afghanistan, an earthquake in Haiti, the crisis at the southern border, climate change, hurricanes, flooding, and inflation—nothing seemed to rouse people's indignation regardless of their political persuasion. Frank found these discussions tiresome and unrewarding. He tried to steer their conversation back to another topic of mutual interest—money.

"I think Vinnie's going to sign with the SPAC later this week," he said.

"How much is he going to get?"

"It looks like about two hundred million."

"With most of that coming from the mob bank, right?" Helen said.

"That's the deal as I understand it. Your Omaha ploy was a brainstorm to start a bidding war, and you had Tony bidding against himself. The way it probably plays out, Vinnie gets the money, but he loses his business; And he's selling it at a big discount. I hope he's happy with that; I've always thought he loved that business."

"You know more about this than I do, but does the mob bank know what they're getting into?"

It's a good question. The SPAC deal is a relatively easy way to go public, but then the new entity has to open its books to regulators just like any public corporation. I'm not sure the folks at Sunshine Investment Bank will be happy with that part, considering where their money comes from."

"What if Vinnie got the money from Tony, and then Sunshine pulled out of the deal?" Helen asked.

"I'm not sure I understand where you're going with this." Frank sipped his wine and began to concentrate on Helen's questions. He sensed that she was hatching a new scheme.

"Well, Tony is the one who's hot to take over Vinnie's operation. Sunshine is just in there to make some quick money. Right?"

"I guess that's right, but I'm not sure Tony wants to get into commercial real estate. He just wants to sell shares and have somebody else run it. I think he's cash-poor right now. Anyway, I'm not sure what you're saying."

"What I'm trying to say, darling, is we could get Tony's money for Vinnie, and at the same time we could get Sunshine to understand the mistake they're about to make. They'd pull out when they realize the feds will be studying their financial books as soon as the deal closes."

"If I understand where you're going, you're cooking up another clandestine operation. The answer is no… absolutely not! Tony's boys may be inept, but those boys in New York and South

Florida are a different breed of cat. You are absolutely not getting involved with them."

"Not me, darling. I'm thinking of Rachel and Moselle. They're both born actors. Plus, Rachel can help the bank's people understand the financial predicament they're getting into."

"I'm glad you're not planning another field trip, but a dust-up with these people is dangerous for everybody." Frank decided to play for time in the hope he could thwart Helen's scheme. "Have you talked to Rachel and Moselle about your idea?"

"Just preliminary conversations at this point. Moselle seems excited about my idea. Rachel still needs a little more convincing. She's the key because she can hack into the bank's files."

"You *know* she's a hacker?"

"Certainly … I've talked to her about this. How do you think she gets all this information about the bank and its directors?"

"I always figured she had some advanced hacking skills or some connections, but I never asked her about it."

"Well … I did. She's found a backdoor into

their files. They don't even know she's a frequent visitor."

Frank marveled at Helen's scheme, but he also worried about the risks of her plan. He particularly did not want to put Moselle and Rachel in harm's way. "Alright, I'll bite," he said. "Tell me how you see your idea playing out."

"You want details or the executive summary?"

"The latter, please."

"First, we have to get Tony to pay Vinnie early. Then Moselle and Rachel talk to the bank. The bank drops out of the deal, and Vinnie has Tony's money."

"And Tony realizes he's been conned again, and we have a homicidal maniac on our hands. I don't want to go through *that* again."

"I've got a plan for that too. Vinnie doesn't really need the money, and you've got plenty. I think we can deal with Tony by making him out to be a philanthropist. He'll love it when the media starts fawning over him. He doesn't know it yet, but he's really going to need some favorable publicity in the near future."

"And what do you mean by that?"

"I mean the feds are closing in on Tony, and his wealthy colleagues in New York and South Florida will be very unhappy with him if my plan works."

Frank felt like the new kid on his first day of school. "And how do you know that?" he asked.

"Part of it is intuition, but this part is a hard fact. The feds are getting ready to bring new indictments about Tony's illegal income."

"I'm afraid to ask how you know that."

"I'm afraid to tell you."

Tony Ragusa knew he had tax troubles. For years he had tried to conceal the illegal income from shakedowns, extortion, and healthcare fraud inside the income reporting for his waste management operation. The scam had worked well until the pandemic happened. Income from waste management had plummeted with the absence of office workers and the effect of the lockdown, and yet his reported income had not changed. In fact, it had increased with income from his successful government fraud operation. The feds meant to distribute large sums during the lockdown for payroll support, and Tony had gotten more than his share of it. The illegal income had become the biggest part of his bottom line, yet he had no choice but to conceal it as income from waste management. The government accountants could be slow, but they were not stupid. They watched his rising income and knew he had income from illicit sources. Other waste management firms had missed their estimates in 2020, and several had gone bankrupt.

Tony figured he needed to do something dramatic to distract attention from his tax situation, and violence had always been the default solution to his problems.

"Old Frank is the key to this thing. He's got the money and he's got Vinnie's back. We get him out of the game; Vinnie can't stand alone," he said to his assistants.

The room was silent as his assistants waited for Tony's newest plan. "Old Frank has a good ground defense. What we need to have now is a little air raid."

"Sir?" said his consigliere, Samuel Mancuso, in alarm.

"Old Frank and his gun moll are out in the middle of nowhere on top of a hill. What we do is we fly some drones into his place; we arm them with light explosives, break a few windows and bring down some plaster. That's enough to put a good scare into old Frank and Annie Oakley."

"Sir, we can't do that now. Our colleagues in New York and Broward County say any violence at this point will nullify our agreement." Sam Mancuso spoke his piece and waited for Tony to explode.

"Huh? You been talking to their bank again?"

"Yes, sir. That's what I've been doing at your direction. We are very close to finishing this deal."

"Sammy, you're a good man, but you got no imagination. I need some original thinking around here and right now."

It was the first time Samuel Mancuso had heard his name spoken with any affection. He managed a smile as he said, "Sir, just a little more patience and we can close this deal. You'll have a big chunk of the commercial real estate operation in Chicago. Just a little more patience is all we need."

"I'll given them another week, but you boys start working on the drone package; maybe strap on some claymores. We'll do it after he signs."

"Well… actually, sir, we think he's ready to sign now. However, he wants a down payment from you."

"A down payment? What're you talking about?"

"He's calling it earnest money. Something in the way of sealing the deal."

"Don't he trust me? There's a catch in here somewhere." Tony's grammar tended to deteriorate when he became agitated.

A rhetorical question about trust usually goes unanswered, and this occasion was no exception. Tony glowered, "Alright, how much does he want?"

"Half of your thirty million buyout. Fifteen million."

"What the hell? I smell a rat in here. Give him a few million before he signs. I'm tired of his stalling."

"I think he'll accept ten million. His people say he wants it to be a simple number."

Tony's eyes narrowed. "Then give him ten. We've been working on this deal forever. I want to close it out."

When they exited Tony's conference room, Sam Mancuso turned to one of his accountants and said *sotto voce,* "I'm thinking he's being conned again. This prepayment smells. He has no idea if Buffet is even involved in this deal. I think he's being played again by that crazy woman he calls Annie Oakley."

"She may be crazy, but I wouldn't want to get in a gunfight with her," replied the accountant.

Chapter 6

As the day of the merger approached, an action the financial people called a De-SPAC, all sides made intense preparations for the big event. Because of Covid restrictions, the closing would be done remotely. Each of the three parties had tirelessly reviewed the documents prepared for the merger. Tony and Vinnie, at separate locations in Chicago, would each sign the agreement, have it immediately notarized, and fax the documents to the other parties. Both Tony and Vinnie would have a pack of lawyers, accountants, and financial advisors nearby. Both men also insisted that one of their lawyers be physically present when the other party signed the documents. The representatives of Sunshine Investment Bank in West Palm Beach, more experienced with the machinations of a SPAC, would simply sign, notarize, and fax the documents to Vinnie and Tony.

Frank was also included in the remote feed at Vinnie's request. Tony consented to this request because he thought Frank was a demented old man and could do no harm. He did insist that Helen not be allowed to witness the proceedings in real time. The reason for his objection to Helen went unstated although it was clear to nearly everyone that Tony feared Helen and hated her for that.

Unbeknownst to Tony or the Sunshine bankers, Rachel and her associates had hacked into the software program for the remote meeting. Helen had offered Moselle and Rachel one hundred thousand dollars each for their roles in the hack. She had also offered Rachel an additional fifty thousand dollars for her technical expertise. The two women assumed that Helen was good for the money because they knew Frank was rich. And Helen had been tutoring Rachel and Moselle on the art of acting. The plan was for the two women to appear remotely to the Sunshine people immediately after the merger happened and the other parties had signed out. The two women would present the data on Tony's precarious financial and legal situation and educate the Sunshine bankers on the regulatory requirements they would face after they took Vinnie's business public. Helen predicted the Sunshine people would back out and leave Tony stranded in a deal he could not complete.

"Don't forget that the gesture should precede the spoken word, and remember you'll be wearing half-face masks," she said. "On the small screen the gesture alerts the viewer to who's talking. You make the gesture, even if it's a little smile, say your piece, and then go to your graphs and charts. You both should rehearse with that in mind. And remember to smile with your eyes."

"How much time will we have?" Moselle said.

"Probably two to three minutes before they cut us off," Rachel replied. "This is a guesstimate based on the previous times it's taken the company to recognize a hack. We shouldn't make our visuals too complicated. Just show them

Ragusa's financial situation and the regulatory hurdles they'll face when the new company goes public. Two graphs or charts should be enough with backup details on your presentations. Remember my program will let you use the laser pointer to drill into details."

"We'll each use one chart," said Moselle. "I'll show them Ragusa's financial situation, and Rachel can explain the regulatory hurdles for the new company. We can do that in two minutes."

"Good," said Helen. "We'll prerecord it, and Rachel can splice it into the hack software. We'll play it as soon as Ragusa signs off. The bankers at Sunshine will not be happy."

୧୬

The singular day of the merger seemed almost anticlimactic. Tony's people had been working on it for over a year, and the people at Sunshine Investment Bank had been poised to supply the money for over six months. Tony's media mavens had done a good job of touting the greenness of the shell company, which they had named Terzo Constructors. Sunlight and wind would power its buildings, and waste would be incinerated and recycled. The video simulations were very convincing. Vinnie had been as evasive as he could, but economics forced all parties to finish the deal. The paperwork was ready, the appropriate forms filed, and tedious preparation for the transition to a public company, Terzo Constructors, was in place.

The parties met remotely. Vinnie was in his office accompanied by lawyers, accountants, and technical people, all wearing masks. Tony was in his conference room with his retinue, some of them masked. The Sunshine interest was represented by two unmasked bankers, who sat in an ornate conference room in West Palm Beach.

A spokeswoman, agreed on by all parties, began to speak when everyone was seated and appeared to be paying attention. "Gentleman, we are here today to do the initial closing. The closing will be followed by a PIPE, a private investment to fund the new public entity. Mr. Ragusa will hold fifteen percent of the equity in the new entity as a favored investor, and Sunshine Investment Bank, as principal source of the private investment, will hold eighty-five percent. Are we agreed so far?"

Heads at all three sites gave affirmative nods. "Let's get this done," Tony growled.

"Good," said the spokeswoman. "Mr. Palermo and Mr. Ragusa, you will each be given multiple papers for signature. Your associates have reviewed these papers, and there are no surprises. Please sign each with your legal name and pass them to the notary. The signed and notarized papers will then be faxed and sent electronically in pdf form to the other parties. I think this process will feel seamless for everyone concerned."

The remote meeting proceeded with Tony grumbling as his assistant placed papers in front of him. The documents were soon signed, notarized, and faxed. When each site confirmed receipt of the documents, the spokeswoman said, "Thank you both. Now the Sunshine representatives will supply copies of their contribution to each of you. Once that is done, I believe these proceedings are complete."

More papers were signed, notarized, and faxed. Tony said, "Alright, Vinnie, it's finally done. I have no beef with you, and I hope we remain on friendly terms. You're selling your company for a fair price, actually for more than I think it's worth. No hard feelings, okay?"

Vinnie nodded affirmatively in a respectful way but remained silent.

The spokeswoman said, "Are there any questions, gentlemen?"

Silence followed and the spokeswoman said, "Hearing none, I would like to congratulate you both on a civil and efficient transaction. These proceedings are adjourned."

Video screens began to go blank, but before the Sunshine bankers could touch their laptops, Rachel's hack appeared on their screens. Moselle, half-masked in simple gold Mardi Gras fashion stood in front of a large chart. She smiled and said, "Good morning, gentlemen. Please note this chart." She stepped aside and continued. "These numbers show Mr. Ragusa's earnings and debt for the last five years. You will note that while his income has increased every year, his debt has grown disproportionately. He is now mortgaged for about ten times his annual income, which includes both reported and unreported sources. These are short-term debts that are coming due weekly. We have obtained these numbers not only from his tax returns but from his own books, and the two do not remotely agree. These figures should be very interesting to the IRS."

Moselle smiled broadly, "You will also receive this information on your laptops and cellphones so please do not worry about the brevity of this presentation. Thank you for your attention. Now my colleague will briefly review some of the issues you may anticipate when Terzo Constructors goes public."

Moselle stepped aside and Rachel appeared on the screen, smiling as the first chart disappeared and a new chart appeared. Her half mask featured feathered eyebrows and tiny eye slits in contrast to the plain golden half-mask worn by Moselle. "Good morning, gentlemen. This chart shows a summary sheet for the IRS form 8K—also called a super 8K. As you know, this information must be disclosed within four days of the launch of your new entity, Terzo Constructors."

❧

The bankers at Sunshine desperately tried to shut down the hack and then realized that they needed to record it. Their laptops had no control of the presentation. Rachel smiled again and said, "Please note section two, financial reporting, and section five, corporate governance."

The two bankers grabbed their cell phones and called their IT department. Rachel continued, "These two sections will require detailed information about your bank and the sources of your financial backing."

The bankers frantically tried to get their IT people on the call. "Don't worry about the details, gentlemen; you both will receive links to our presentations on your laptops and cell phones. Let me drill down on sections two and five. The super 8K form you must file will require information about your assets, including information on your major depositors. I'm sure many of your depositors would prefer that their identities and assets remain confidential. You may want to rethink Sunshine's role in this SPAC. Thank you for your attention."

The bankers' laptops went dark, and then links appeared to the presentations given by Moselle and Rachel. The two bankers sat in stunned silence. Finally, one said, "Download everything in those links. I'll call New York and Hallandale. We've got a big problem here. It looks like Ragusa didn't level with us, and I'm thinking somebody's been into our files."

Moselle and Rachel had nurtured the seeds of doubt in the minds of the Sunshine bankers, and their further probing of the links provided by the two women only confirmed their suspicions that Tony Ragusa was not a truthful man. Information from the links was quickly communicated to their superiors in New York City and Hallandale Beach in Broward County. Back came instructions to avoid any further participation in the SPAC merger. This action effectively isolated Tony Ragusa and his machinations to merge with Vinnie's company. His financial support had disappeared.

Rachel's video hack could not be retrieved nor traced. It had disappeared as soon as it played, but the links remained available. That information with its underlying computer code was quickly forwarded to the bank's hackers in Belarus. A thorough scouring of this data did not reveal its author initially, but suspicions centered on Vinnie Palermo and his uncle, Frank Palermo, for want of more likely suspects.

More time elapsed before the Sunshine bankers and their sponsors concluded that someone had not only hacked Tony's finances but had also gotten into the bank's confidential records. The seriousness of this intrusion made them redouble their efforts to identify the hacker, and the bank's team of hackers in Belarus began to report some progress in identifying the source of the hack and who was behind it.

❧

Vinnie had watched the hack as it played. "Will you look at that?" he said, "I can't believe how much information she had on Tony's debts. That girl is a genius, but I hope she knows what she's gotten into." He called Frank to discuss their plans.

Frank hadn't seen the hack, but he had witnessed the rehearsals so often that he had memorized the presentations. "I think it went well, Vinnie. I don't see Sunshine continuing to support this SPAC."

"Frank, don't you think Helen's gone too far with this thing? She'll not only have Tony after her, but Sunshine's principals will figure out someone's been into their confidential files."

"Vinnie, this is a good deal for you. You've got Tony's money and you'll likely keep your business."

"I don't want Tony's money. That little *teppista* is crazy. Mark my words, he'll try to kill us all."

"I think we can head him off on that. Helen has a plan. We just need to buy some time for him to cool off after the New York and South Florida people talk some sense into him. Why don't you offer to give him back his money?"

"Give it back? The hell you say! It was a business deal. He knew what he was doing when he advanced the money. It was earnest money. I'm keeping it."

Frank knew that Vinnie didn't actually possess Tony's earnest money from the SPAC deal, a fact that Vinnie had apparently forgotten. Tony's ten million dollar advance had gone into an LLC that Frank had set up and that remained under his control. The plan had been to hold the money there in case the deal fell apart.

Tony's exploded in rage when he learned about the hack. "What? What are you talking about? Someone has been into our records?"

"Yes, sir," said his consigliere, "We learned about it this morning from New York. Apparently, the hacker had access to our records as well as the bank's records."

"Let me get this straight. You're saying the hacker has our financial records … the ones we don't report?"

"That seems to be the case. We are waiting to get access to the links the hackers furnished to the bank, but it looks like our multiple income disparities are out there now for everyone to see."

Tony's face reddened as he pounded his desk. "It's that goddam woman again, Annie Oakley. I know it's her. She's married to old Frank. I can't remember her name. What's her name?"

"Actually, sir, from what we've learned so far, she was not on the video hack. It was two young women—one Black, both evidently American. They were wearing half-masks. And the name in question is Helen Cohen Palermo."

"I don't care. I know who's behind this. I can smell her stink in this. She's gone too far this time. She's ruined my deal."

The consigliere, Samuel Mancuso, sighed and waited for Tony's next explosion before telling him another thing he would not want to hear.

"I'll kill all of them for this. It's the least they deserve for what they've done to me. And I'm going to enjoying doing it."

"Sir, our New York and Broward County colleagues are requesting that you fly down and meet them in Nassau. They want to talk to you about this matter."

Chapter 7

The 'requests' given Tony were clear and succinct. He was to fly to Nassau on Saturday, September 11th, accompanied only his consigliere, Samuel Mancuso. They would enter Sunshine Investment Bank's conference room at precisely 10:45 a.m. EDT in preparation for a short meeting with representatives of the New York City and South Florida families, who would arrive at eleven o'clock sharp. No one would bring weapons or recording devices.

Tony did as he was instructed, but stormy weather on their route delayed his plane, causing him to arrive at the bank at 11:15 a.m. After they were frisked and x-rayed, Tony and Sam entered the conference room to face five old men, who were already seated. "You're late," said Vito Ragusa, acting street boss of the Genovese family in New York. "It's not a good way to start a meeting like this. And don't think you being my cousin will help you here."

Tony mumbled something about bad weather and took a seat. He knew it was a bad start. "Please let me just say —"

"We did not invite you here to talk, only to listen. Now shut up and start doing that," said Vito Ragusa.

Tony was silent and tried to act respectful and even contrite, although he was not known for either trait. He did his best to strike an appropriate pose but found it difficult. Sam sat immobile and silent

"Tony, you fed us lies about your finances, and you disobeyed our request that you refrain from violent activities. We have divorced ourselves from your SPAC plan completely. You're on your own. You can proceed as you wish, but don't involve us and don't expect any help from us."

"But I'm out fifteen million, Vito. Vinnie Palermo has my fifteen million." Tony had inflated the amount of his earnest money.

"*Sei un cannone scolioto,*" said Pasquale Salerno, acting underboss of the South Florida faction. "We wash our hands of you. You've caused our bank files to be compromised. You have no idea how much trouble you've caused us."

"My finances have been hacked too."

"We know that, and it's your problem alone. We will repair our damages without any more involvement from you. We don't care what happens to you, but you will regret it if you cause us any more problems."

A brief silence offered Tony the opportunity to defend himself again. "Let me just—"

"*Stai, zitto!*" said another acting underboss from one of the five New York families. "The meeting is finished. It was foolish of us to try to work with you. We are divorcing you. Let us never hear from you again."

"I want my break-up fee. I brought this deal to you, and now you're backing out. You owe me the break-up fee, and you know it."

"Just get out, Tony," said Patsy Salerno. "This meeting is over, and we're through with you."

Tony and his consigliere rose and left the room. Tony was muttering as they walked out into the bright Bahamian sunshine. "*Cazzo*, they're all *cazzo*. I wash my hands of them too. They have the *testicoli* to lecture me after all I've done for them. They can all go to hell for what I care."

Sam Mancuso was unaware that Tony had ever done anything of value for their New York and South Florida associates, but he kept silent. The flight back to Chicago was marked by Tony drinking several glasses of Scotch and ranting wildly about the revenge he would exact on Vinnie Palermo and his family. Upon landing in Chicago, Sam drove Tony to their office building and gave him two Valiums.

Tony later took Prozac and Sonata capsules with another glass of Scotch before trying to get some sleep. He had seen a doctor once about his problems with sleep. The visit had consisted of a long interview, the completion of several questionnaires, an examination, and several blood tests. Afterwards, the doctor advised against using alcohol and sleeping pills and wanted to treat him with lithium for something he called a bipolar disorder, whatever the hell that was. Tony thought lithium was good for batteries, not for sleep. He decided he didn't need a quack doctor for sleep; he needed a better pill.

In reality, as his financial situation deteriorated, he had begun to increasingly self-medicate. He sensed that his life was unraveling. His wife had moved out of their large Northshore home, taking their two children. He dreaded going to his empty home, and he was spending his days and nights at his office building in River North.

&

Rachel Bruggeman had a small corner office in Wildwood, Missouri, set quietly among upscale restaurants and boutiques. The development was in the new style of an outdoor mall built in clusters. Her plaque on the office door said Bruggemann and Associates – Accounting and Investigations. No one in the nearby stores had ever seen an associate, and, in fact, few had seen Rachel. She parked her Tesla sedan behind her office very early every morning and entered through the secured back door. She left the office before noon every day as quietly as she had arrived. The front door was kept locked. The few people who actually visited her office came by appointment and were admitted by Rachel. By all accounts, Rachel was the only person in her office.

Rachel had operated in this manner until the SPAC deal with Sunshine Bank had evaporated in Tony Ragusa's face. At that point, Helen insisted that Rachel give her a magnetic key to the back door and have a confidential way to contact her. Helen didn't think Tony would do much because she figured he had been chastised by his New York and South Florida associates, but she wanted Rachel to have some back up. Helen's home in St. Albans was only about ten minutes away from Rachel's office, and Helen promised to respond immediately when contacted by a pre-arranged text to her phone.

One crisp autumn morning Rachel was surprised to see two men enter her office through the front door. "How did you get in here?" she asked in alarm.

"We obviously came in through your front door," one said.

Rachel studied the two men, who were not wearing masks. They were middle-aged, well groomed, and immaculately clad. She liked men, especially when they were clean and wore expensive clothing. On these two, she guessed Canali suits and Ferragamo shoes. Maybe the suit on the tall one was from Brioni, or even was a bespoke creation from a Milan tailor. They looked like slick Italian editions of successful Wall Street bankers except they were also vaguely menacing. "I'm asking how you got in the front door."

"With a duplicate of your magnetic key. We wanted you to know that we can hack too."

"Please state your business. What do you want?" Rachel sat down and turned on her desktop lamp, which sent the alerting text to Helen's phone.

"Our bank's cybersecurity department is impressed with your skills in accessing the confidential electronic files of our clients."

"I farm out most of that work."

"We know you do. So do we. It turns out we have common friends in eastern Europe."

Rachel was alarmed but she tried to remain composed. She knew she needed to stall for time. These two intruders were clearly not low-level gangsters, but they frightened her. "Besides being impressed, what do you want?" She hoped Helen would be true to her word.

"We are here to offer you a consulting contract," said the shorter man. "You tell us how you penetrated our security firewall, and we pay you a consulting fee."

"I don't sign contracts."

"It's a handshake deal without the handshake," the taller man said as he placed a thumb drive on her desk. "You'll find a website on here with a link to a bank draft for twenty-five thousand dollars, payable to you."

Rachel inserted the drive and fiddled with the instructions on the website, working as slowly as she thought appeared plausible. Soon enough Helen let herself in through the back door and stood beside Rachel. Rachel noticed that Helen wore black silk slacks and a white knit top, St. John she guessed. The Sig-Sauer rested in a fast-draw holster on Helen's right hip, clearly visible. Her arms were relaxed, her right hand within inches of the gun.

Both men raised their hands in mock surrender. "We don't want any trouble. We aren't carrying firearms."

"We don't want any trouble either," Helen said. "Is everything okay here, Rachel?"

"Yes, thank you, Helen," Rachel said. "These gentlemen have come here with a business proposition. If everyone will keep their hands where I can see them and not do anything rash, I would like to check out the full contents of this thumb drive."

She opened the link and transferred the bank draft to her private account in a Cayman Islands bank. She then downloaded another link to the thumb drive before she raised her eyes to her two visitors, who had found seats across from her desk. Helen continued to stand beside Rachel. "I just placed a link on your thumb drive that will take you to a full explanation of the protocol we used to penetrate your files." She handed over the thumb drive. "I've been expecting you… or someone like you. I must say I'm impressed with your alacrity and efficiency."

"May we check the link before we leave?" one asked.

"No, you should leave now. The link that I have provided is valid. You will see how we modified a widely available cybersecurity evaluation program for our purposes. You may do what you want with it; we'll never use it again."

Helen and her Sig-Sauer were very persuasive. The shorter man pocketed the thumb drive, and they exited through the front door. Rachel rose and threw the door's deadbolt behind them. Then she wedged a chair against the door handle. "So much for my security," she said. "Thank you for coming, Helen. Those two scared me. I clearly need to upgrade my systems."

"Are you sure you want to work with those people?" Helen asked.

"I think this was a one-off transaction. They acted like perfect gentlemen, and I liked the way they dress, especially the tall one. But I wouldn't want to work with them long-term. I did not consider them friendly."

"Frank says they're all dangerous."

"I'm sure they are. Nearly everyone is dangerous these days with the virus and all, don't you think?"

Helen sensed that Rachel's bravado was forced, but she smiled and said nothing further.

ↄ

Two days later Rachel met with Helen and Frank at their home on Wings Road above St. Albans. They usually met remotely, but Rachel had requested the personal meeting. They sat on the terrace and enjoyed a lovely fall morning marked by soft sunshine and low humidity. "Thank you for letting me visit," she said after taking a seat. "Your home is beautiful and what a view you have."

"Frank found it. We're out in the country a little too much for my taste, but we feel safe here." Cane, their Australian Shepherd walked over and sniffed Rachel's hand. The dog was no longer a puppy but not yet fully grown. After investigating Rachel, Cane found a shady spot on the terrace and took up his sentinel duties.

Rachel smiled thinly and said, "I just wanted to meet with you because those two uninvited visitors to my office have really unnerved me. I'm also worried about what's happened with the SPAC and what I'm guessing Mr. Ragusa's response will be. I think he is a violent person."

"You're right about that," Frank said, "but he seems to be growing more erratic. At my insistence, Vinnie offered to return half of advance yesterday, and Tony refused it. He said it's not about money, it's about trust and respect."

"Trust is not one of Tony's strong points," Helen said. "I wonder if he's ever trusted anyone, and I doubt anyone trusts him."

"I believe he will eventually accept the money," Frank said, "and I think Vinnie will give it all back if Tony meets him halfway. The partial return was an initial offer."

"I'm not sleeping at night, worrying about this," Rachel said. "When we did the video, I thought it was all a lark, but I've come to realize I shouldn't have gone out front on this. I'm a back-office person. That's where I've always been happy. Now I'm in trouble with a mob bank in Florida and Tony Ragusa in Chicago."

"You can come stay with us for a while, if that will help," Helen said. "We've got good security here and plenty of room."

"All of my work is done at my office. I have to go there because, well… that's where all my hardware and software is. I thought my operation was secure until those two men walked in. Now the more I think about what's happening, I've gotten frightened."

"Security is a relative word," Frank said. He had once read that in a newspaper article about cybersecurity and was trying to sound smart. "I tell you what. You should secure your office operation as best you can and stay with us for a while. We'll ask Barney to accompany you to your office and back every day. He brings about as much security to the party as any one man I know."

Rachel thanked them for their offer of hospitality and security and said she would think about it. When she walked out, Cane followed her. The dog sat at the end of the driveway and watched her car until it disappeared down the hill.

Helen looked at Frank and said, "I misjudged her. I thought she could handle being on stage, but she's more of a backstage person. I shouldn't have encouraged her to appear on the video hack."

"Don't beat up on yourself. She puts herself out there as a hacker, she's got to expect some downside. She's still young. Her skin will get thicker."

"Never mind her skin; it would be better if she bought some body armor," Helen said. "She's going to be in real trouble if Tony finds out who she is, and I don't think she can handle it."

That's only the second time I've heard you admit that you might have made a mistake in judging someone," Frank said.

"It wasn't a mistake; it was a miscalculation. I can see that she's very vulnerable now and unsure about what to do next. She needs to be strengthened."

"God help her if you start doing that," Frank said.

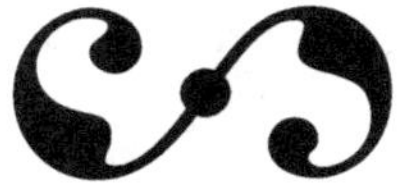

Chapter 8

Rachel called them the next morning and accepted their offer of security and a temporary place to stay. When she appeared that evening, she brought two suitcases and six pantsuits. Cane gave an excited yelp and ran two circles around her. "Thank you again for your offer," she said. "I assume Barney is agreeable with this plan."

"He's happy to help you," Helen said as she accompanied Rachel to the far guest room. "He'll drive behind you to work every day and be there to follow you when you're finished. We don't have a rapid charging station for your Tesla, but Frank will have one installed."

"Thank you, but it's not necessary. I have one at work that I can use."

"We'll put one in here anyway. I'm guessing the charging station near your office doesn't offer much security. You've got to be careful in today's world. Anyway, I think our next car will be electric."

"Your dog seems to like me. He really is a handsome boy with those blue eyes."

"It's characteristic of the breed. I picked Cane out of his litter because it looked like he would have the bluest eyes."

As if on cue, Cane began following Rachel throughout the house. At night when she retired, he slept at the foot of her bed. The next morning, he followed her down the front sidewalk and jumped across the driver's seat when she opened her car door. He positioned himself on the passenger side and looked back at her as if to say, 'let's go.'

Helen who had accompanied Rachel to the car said, "I think he's adopted you. Why don't you take him to your office with you? But I have to warn you, he needs exercise. He's bred as a herding dog."

Rachel smiled at Helen and said, "This dog may turn out to be the best boyfriend I've ever had. The previous ones set the bar pretty low. You don't mind if I take him to work?"

"I think he's already settled that question. Cane is a very smart dog. If he likes you, you've got a friend for life."

Rachel and Cane became inseparable. He shadowed her day and night, and she raced him around the yard when they returned from work. They only stopped running together when they both could run no more. In this way, they got their exercise and stayed fit. She fed him twice daily and walked him when he signaled his needs to her. He still lived with Helen and Frank, but he had become Rachel's dog ... or maybe she had become Cane's deputy.

ɔ

In Chicago, Tony Ragusa's impulse control unraveled further. His associates could see that he was drinking during the day, a behavior he could hide when he was drinking only at home. Now that he was living in his office building, his use of alcohol and prescription drugs became obvious to everyone around him. He was clearly angry about the collapse of his SPAC deal to take over Vinnie Palermo's business, and the weight of his increasing business debts made his situation even more stressful. He had borrowed large sums of money and mortgaged his assets to expand his waste disposal business just before the pandemic began to unfold. The resulting lockdown severely depressed his commercial waste disposal business. He had debts he simply could not pay, and his precarious financial situation had been exposed by the hack of his confidential files. Tony was obsessed with finding the hacker. He also felt he was owed a break-up fee of fifteen million dollars from Sunshine Investment Bank on the SPAC debacle. The deal was a handshake agreement, but Tony believed he was owed the money because he had brought the deal to the bank. The bankers at Sunshine disputed this and refused to pay. Their lawyers maintained that Tony had negated the entire deal when he had misrepresented his financial situation to them. Because of their particular histories, neither party could take the matter to court. They had to find other ways to settle their dispute.

His weekly staff meeting brought more bad news. The federal payroll support program was winding down, diminishing another source of income. "What are you guys doing with the drones?" he asked. "I told you to get me a package worked up. We're hitting Vinnie's office and old Frank's house. This can't be hard. Do I have to do this myself?"

Sam Mancuso could see that Tony was sweating profusely. "Sir, we have those packages about ready, but are you sure this is the way to go on this?"

Tony gave Sam a baleful glare, then collected himself and smiled. "Sammy, you're a good man, but you don't see the big picture. These people have screwed us. They've put my business in the toilet. We've lost respect in New York and South Florida all because of this hacker. I want to know who the goddam hacker is. Was it the woman on the video or somebody else?"

"We think it was one of the women in the video. Our sources at Sunshine Bank now tell us she set up the intrusion with help from a hacker network in Belarus."

"What's her name?"

"We think it's Rachel Bruggemann. She's an accountant in St. Louis…claims she's a forensic accountant."

"What the hell is that?"

"Somebody who traces money…finds out where it's coming from and where's it going—sees if it's on the level. They mostly work with lawyers."

"The bank got hacked too. What're they doing about it?"

"They found this Rachel Bruggemann and talked to her, and she helped them patch their security holes. They think they've persuaded her to lay off their operation. At least that's what they say."

"Why didn't they just take her out after she spilled the beans to them?"

"That was their intention after they got what they wanted. Then Helen Palermo showed up, and they had to leave before they could finish the job."

"Annie Oakley, huh? Why didn't I think of that? That broad pops everywhere I look."

"We think she might be the brains behind Vinnie Palermo's operation at this point."

"Vinnie must be hard up for brains. Where's this hacker now?"

"She has a small office west of St. Louis. She's living with Frank and Helen Palermo in a tiny little town out there."

"Isn't that convenient? I can kill two birds with one drone. You get it…two birds with one drone? Let's get this air raid going." Tony was highly amused at his cleverness.

Sam Mancuso smiled at the riff on the old cliché, but he was not happy. Tony's erratic behavior had brought confusion to their business operations in River North. The situation was vexing enough that Sam had begun to worry about his personal wellbeing. He had opened private communications with his New York and South Florida colleagues to try to insure his survival. He also tried to steer Tony away from an attack on Vinnie's office in the Hancock Building. There were too many people there with a high probability of collateral damage. Attacking the Palermo compound in St. Albans also seemed like a bad idea, but it was probably more feasible with less possibility of collateral damage.

Sam had learned that Tony wasn't the only one having problems with the hack. Sunshine Investment Bank was losing business. South American drug profits had found a lucrative parking place in the bank. With the hack of all the bank's files, these depositors had lost confidence and withdrawn their money. In addition, other clients who brought in deposits had become wary of the bank. The situation was sufficiently serious that the New York and South Florida factions were meeting in Nassau to figure a way to stem the withdrawals. This unusual meeting occurred in the bank's ornate conference room, the one where just a few weeks earlier these same people had so cavalierly dismissed Tony Ragusa. The underbosses had become the decision makers because a number of the top positions in their organizations were vacant. Death, age, debility, and imprisonment had taken their toll. The replacement leadership found their new authority to be a daunting responsibility.

Patsy Salerno of the South Florida group had called the meeting and he spoke first. "We're in a bind here. Our depositors are fleeing. We're getting no new business. We've got to stop the bleeding. I'm opening it up for ideas here."

"We're all having cash flow problems," said Vito Ragusa, "but the loss of the South American money is a big blow. We've got to stop the bleeding."

Other underbosses agreed that the bleeding must be stopped, but no one offered a remedy.

Finally, Patsy Salerno tried to focus their minds. "We need to do something definite. I think we should hit Tony Rags. He's the one that got us into this mess." After further chatter, the others began to agree.

Vito Ragusa questioned how a hit would benefit the bank, and Patsy attempted to explain. "If Tony gets hit and people know it was us, it'll build confidence that we did something. Our depositors will come back. People will know we aren't pushovers. New business will flow to us again."

"What about the hacker?" a New York acting underboss asked.

"We found her, and she cooperated with us. She helped us patch holes in our cybersecurity that we didn't know existed. I think we have her under control.

"She's the one that really screwed us. I think she needs to pay for this," said another acting New York underboss.

"I don't think she's going to be a problem for us. Please remember she's close to Frank Palermo."

"Who?"

"Frank Palermo. He's Vinnie Palermo's uncle. We think he's the money behind Vinnie's business. Warren Buffett was never involved in this crazy deal that Tony got us into."

"We don't control Vinnie Palermo's operation," said a New York acting street boss.

"Remember we thought we controlled Tony, and that turned out to be wrong. I am beginning to think Vinnie is the only sane man in Chicago. He's close enough to us that I believe we can work with him."

"Assassinations are out of style," said another street boss from New York. "There are much cleaner ways to do this now. Our friends in eastern Europe can make it look like a heart attack, and we can still say it was us. That way the cops don't come looking for us ... at least not right away."

This idea was generally endorsed. Patsy, who had become their leader by default, assigned duties and scheduled another meeting in Nassau in two weeks. The meeting adjourned and its participants departed on their planes for New York and Broward County.

ℭ

Unhappiness had also begun to permeate Frank and Helen's house. When Rachel and Cane departed to her office every morning, the couple argued about Rachel. At first Frank was puzzled, but as he listened to Helen, a common thread emerged. Helen always returned to her objections to Rachel as their continued houseguest.

"I like Rachel, but she's taken over our lives," Helen said. "She's even taken our dog. I don't see why she can't stay with Moselle and Barney. They've got room."

"My dear, you're the one who invited her. If I didn't know better, I'd think you're jealous."

"I'm not jealous! But I didn't marry you to have an attractive young woman running around my house half-dressed every morning."

"I'll ask her to wear a housecoat when she comes to breakfast. I think the idea that Rachel is interested in me is laughable. I'm an ugly old man. She couldn't see anything in me."

"You're not ugly, and you must know there's one clear reason why she's interested in you."

Frank recognized that Helen was talking about his money—an undeniable fact. It made their lives more bearable, but it attracted attention and envy. And it now seemed to be driving a wedge into their marriage.

"Helen, you've divorced two husbands and buried a third," he said. "I really want to make this marriage work. I'll check with Barney. He didn't take the job with us to include houseguests. I never thought of that. I'll have to talk to him."

"You'd better check with Moselle. I've already talked to her, and I think she's agreeable. And Cane will be nearby. It's a good solution to the problem. Everybody will be happy. And I didn't divorce two husbands; they divorced me."

Frank realized Helen had solved a problem that he didn't know existed. Rachel could sense Helen's increasing discomfort, and she moved in with Moselle and Barney the next day.

Chapter 9

When Tony's men stole a shipment of Sig-Sauer handguns from a U.S. Army supply depot in the Southside of Chicago a year earlier, they also picked up a batch of C-4 plastic explosives and several claymore mines. The handguns were immediately useful for their shakedown and extortion activities, but the utility of the C-4 and claymores was not initially evident. Tony had them store the ordnance for future use. He said you never know when you might need to make a bomb.

As Tony's fortunes deteriorated with the failed SPAC effort, and the hack of his financial situation, the future had arrived. He plotted to use the ordnance to kill Helen and Rachel in the house high above St. Albans. His men had found a former South American drug cartel member, who knew how to arm and fly explosive-laden drones to specific targets. Sam Mancuso had dissuaded Tony from bombing Vinnie's office in downtown Chicago because of the high likelihood of collateral damage, but the isolated house above St. Albans offered a rich target for a precision strike.

After several meetings with the bomber, Tony was convinced his plan would work. "You can fly these things across the river and pinpoint their house, right?" he said.

"*Si, Senor*… uh, yes, sir, Mr. Ragusa. We can even target rooms in the house if you wish."

Tony was studying an aerial photograph of the house. "Good, I want to hit the bedrooms where the hacker sleeps and where Annie Oakley will be."

"If you hit Helen Palermo, you'll also hit Frank Palermo," Sam said.

"So what? I hate both of those women, and I want to be sure I get them. If old Frank goes down, that's not my problem. I want to hit them late at night when I'm sure where they'll be."

The bomber seemed very confident. "My quadcopters with have video cameras and remote detonators. We can fly them into the bedroom windows and detonate the claymores and C-4 with directional blasts. Nobody in those rooms can survive that."

"Perfect! I love it. I want you to do it early next Sunday morning. This will settle two scores for me."

Sam thought this plan was particularly misguided, but he kept silent. To blow up a private home was unwise in itself, but to meet with the potential bomber several times in this public way left an evidence trail that would be difficult to erase. He knew he would have to talk to his colleagues on the East Coast about what would soon transpire. He had been communicating with Vito Ragusa and Pasquale Salerno through an encrypted link on his home computer, and he passed on this new information. When Vito and Patsy learned about the planned killings, they were as alarmed as Sam, but they saw no way to interrupt the plan in advance without revealing Sam as their source of information. They decided to let the plan proceed. The only part of the plan they liked was the killing of Rachel Bruggemann, an act that their men had intended when they visited her office only to be interrupted by Helen's sudden appearance. The two assassins had been ordered to strangle her and make it look like a rape/murder after they had extracted the desired information about the cybersecurity hack.

ᴄ⌥

Barney Browning knew that their compound atop Wings Road in St. Albans had been under recent drone surveillance. He had installed a radar system that detected low altitude aerial vehicles within a radius of six kilometers. He had also pulled his old Browning semi-automatic, twelve-gauge shotgun out of storage and bought a supply of #8 birdshot. The radar would give him several minutes warning of an impending attack; he was confident he could shoot down attacking drones with his shotgun. It would be like skeet shooting in slow motion.

"We're getting a lot of drone activity around here," he said to Frank. "I'm sure something's about to pop."

"What do you think is going on?"

"I can't pinpoint it, but it's beginning to look like somebody is flying drones across the river at us. It would be relatively simple to arm those drones and attack us from the air."

"That somebody sounds like Ragusa."

"I think so too. It would probably be better if you and Mrs. Palermo moved into the inn down the hill for a few days."

"Not yet. Let's wait and see how this plays out. I don't want to alarm Helen until it's necessary."

"I don't think we'll get much warning, Frank. It looks like they're about ready to act."

Frank pondered his strange situation. In one year, he had gone from an anonymous nobody living quietly in a memory support center to a well-known wealthy man hunted by the Chicago outfit and hated by half the mobsters on the East Coast. His marriage to Helen had brought him to this new reality, and the publicity about his wealth had gained him power and notoriety. He had not been 'made' in the Mafia sense, but he had become marked. He was beginning to feel like a target.

"I'll ask Helen to move into the inn for a few days. I'm staying here. I'm not letting them take down my home without a fight."

"Do you have a weapon?"

"Just some kitchen knives."

"They won't be any good against a drone attack. I'll get you a twenty-gauge with a spread pattern and some birdshot. That's the best way to knock these things out of the sky if you don't have an eagle or a big hawk on retainer."

"I've never shot a gun, but I'll defend my home."

"You're the boss, so you can do what you want, but I think you're taking an unnecessary risk. I'm glad we got Rachel off the top of the hill. I think it's going to get hot up here. I'm putting Moselle in the inn for a few days.

"Moselle actually does what you tell her?"

"Sometimes she does, sometimes not."

"What about Rachel?"

"She wants to stay put. The inn doesn't like dogs, and that dog goes wherever she goes. I've got her sleeping in the basement. It has a walkout door leading down the hill away from the direction the drones will likely come. I'll get her out of the house the minute I know something's up. I think we've got this thing wired."

"I'm thinking I need to build a bomb shelter."

"I'm afraid you don't have time for that. Anyway, you already have a safe room."

&c

The Eastern European consultants with Sunshine Investment Bank worked mainly out of Belarus. These people had many skills and access to even more talent. They could hack almost any electronic file no matter how strong its firewall. If the hacked file could not be sold, they would demand ransom for its return, which they always wanted paid in cryptocurrency. They could then move the digital money around the world and make it eventually appear as a real currency in any offshore bank account. If you hired them, they could even build an electronic trail substantiating that your new money had come to you in a legitimate business transaction. Their services were expensive and in high demand, but assassination was not their strong suite. They had to farm out that task to their colleagues in the Russian Republic.

This they did when the request came through to kill Tony Ragusa in a particular way. Deliberations centered on a quick cause of death that would look natural. Ricin, novichok and cyanide were likely candidates. The problem with the first two poisons was that residue could be detected with a thorough post-mortem examination. Plus, you had to be very careful with either agent or you could kill yourself as quickly as your intended victim. The Russian mobsters didn't like cyanide because it still reminded them of the frustrating way German spies had committed suicide when arrested in World War II. Propofol was a likely candidate, but it had to be given intravenously to be effective. After due consideration, the assassination team chose to use carfentanil, an extremely potent derivative of fentanyl. This narcotic was readily available on the street and inexpensive. A quick spray of carfentanil into the victim's nose stopped respiration and caused death within minutes. Tony was reported to be an abuser of alcohol and prescription drugs, and little suspicion would be aroused if a small amount of this drug showed up in a post-mortem. But you had to be careful with carfentanil. If a tiny amount got into your nose, the same thing could happen to you. The assassins would wear surgical masks and full-face shields when they applied it. They also would carry the opiate antidote, naloxone, and be very quick about their business.

The assassins planned to enter Tony's office building after midnight on a weekend. Sam Mancuso would dismiss Tony's bodyguards at midnight as usual and signal the killers when Tony had fallen asleep. He would give them entrance to the building and then go home to leave the assassins to their task. The Russian mob wanted one hundred thousand dollars to do this job, half of it payable in advance. The bankers at Sunshine and their principals considered this fee to be a bargain and transferred the first payment to a bank account in Malta. The only problem with the plan was bureaucratic inertia. By the time the plan had been formulated in Russia, approved in several locations in the States, and the money transferred to a numbered account in a Maltese bank, Tony had launched his air raid.

☙

The first Saturday in October was a beautiful autumn day in St. Albans—warm and dry with a gentle breeze from the northwest. Frank and Helen entertained their friends and employees with a late luncheon on their terrace. Frank had prepared some snacks, and copious amounts of Italian wine and beer were served. The small gathering expressed a happy and carefree mood although Barney did not drink anything alcoholic. He confined himself to San Pellegrino. Rachel chased Cane around the lawn under the warm sun. Helen, Moselle, and Frank talked freely and drank cold white wine. The golfers looked tiny in the valley below them, and the towboats and barges made their way on the distant river to the west.

As the little party wound down, Moselle said, "Thank you so much for inviting us up here today. The late afternoon sun casts beautiful shadows and colors this time of year. Your home is beautiful, and the view is fantastic."

"I love it out here in the early evening, especially on a day like this," Helen said. "Frank and Barney have us all running scared. I'll be glad when this thing is over, whatever it is they're expecting."

Frank tried to smile, and Barney said, "I think we'll be through this in a few days. We just don't want to take any chances."

Moselle, Rachel, and Barney repeated their thanks and took their leave. Helen and Frank sat on the patio and watched sunset over the vineyards across the river. The floodplain on the far side was littered with wooden flotsam from recent rains, and a few leaves on the trees and vines had begun to turn into brilliant reds and yellows. "Your snacks were delicious, and you still know your wines. I could stay here tonight, or you could come stay with me at the inn," Helen said. "I miss you."

"I miss you, too, but Barney thinks this thing will break soon. You should be at the inn when it happens. I've arranged security down there for you, and you'll be safe. I want to be here to help." Frank did not mention the shotgun he had placed in the utility room closet.

After sunset Helen drove down to the inn in St. Albans. Frank took a short nap and then cleaned up after the party. He played a series of Mozart piano concertos. He called them the four twenties—21, 23, 26 and 27. Mozart was his favorite composer, and he heard something new every time he listened to this music. He fell asleep about eleven o'clock with the loaded shotgun across his lap.

The two bombers drove their Jeep Cherokee off Highway 94 and onto the flood plain across the river at about one a.m. They unloaded four large quadcopter drones with a C-4 package secured on each underside and a claymore opposite it on the other underside. They checked the remote detonators and the video cameras and did several final airworthiness tests of their rigs at very low altitude. At about two a.m., they launched the drones in earnest and began to fly them across the river toward the house on the bluff.

Barney's radar had not detected the short test flights, but alarms sounded immediately when the drones were over the river. He signaled Rachel to evacuate down the hill. He called and texted Frank, picked up his shotgun and night glasses and ran to the terrace of Frank's house.

Tony had chosen a night with a new moon—a tiny crescent-shaped sliver of light in the eastern sky. The drones were silent and had no running lights, but Barney could clearly see them as dark forms against the lighter background of the night sky. When Frank joined him, he said, "There are four of them. You take the one on the far right. I'll take the other three. Wait for my signal before you shoot."

"I can't see them," Frank said.

"Where are your night glasses?"

"I must have left them inside."

"Go get them. You've still got time."

Frank scrambled away and found his night glasses. When he returned, Barney oriented him to the approaching forms. "Do you see them now?"

"I think so. How high are they?"

"They're almost level with us." Barney pointed out over the river, and Frank struggled to locate his target.

"They're just about here; get ready. Raise your gun now!"

"I think I see them," Frank said.

"Fire now!" Barney said. Fire erupted three times from his shotgun, and the sound of the blasts echoed down the bluff toward the river. He hit three drones in succession, and they crashed harmlessly into the bluff below them, setting off fiery explosions on impact. Frank fired into the air and missed his target. Barney trained his gun on the fourth target, but he was too late. The drone slammed into the window of Rachel's bedroom and set off a loud explosion, followed by secondary shrieking noises as the claymore spewed its shrapnel into the room. Smoke and flames jetted out of the bedroom window.

"Quick," Barney said. "We've got to put out the fire." They ran into the house, grabbed fire extinguishers from the hall and put out the flames in the bedroom, which was completely wrecked. The furniture and bed had been destroyed and the wall opposite the window was shredded with the shrapnel from the claymore.

"I'm sorry; I forgot my night glasses. We lost valuable time because of me."

"Don't worry about it. The damage can be

repaired. We're just lucky Rachel wasn't in there."

Frank began to apologize again, but Barney interrupted him. "I think you should sleep in the safe room tonight. I believe that's the end of the action here, but I'll stand guard just in case. I'm sure security with be up here in just a few minutes. I'll handle them. You try to get some sleep."

"Shouldn't we go over there and try to find them?"

"We'd be wasting our time. By the time we got there, they'd be long gone. Maybe we'll find something on the surveillance tapes, but I doubt it. We'll drive over there tomorrow and see if we can find anything, but I doubt that too. These boys were pros. I wasn't expecting four drones. They meant to kill all three of you. I underestimated them. If there's any fault to be found, it's mine."

Chapter 10

The nighttime air raid and bombing energized the sleepy village of St. Albans with feverish talk and wild rumors, and it revived earlier innuendos about Helen and Frank. In the opinion of many, the two were known to be trigger happy since the shooting at the casino hotel. The current incident simply proved it. Never mind that the hotel shooting had been in self-defense and that Helen had not been present during the drone attack on her home on Wings Road. The received opinion was that Helen and Frank attracted violence, that their continued presence in St. Albans was a menace to the little community. A few intrepid souls defended them, but the general presumption was condemnatory and fearful. Suspicion even spread to Moselle and Barney for their association with Helen and Frank.

Rachel was particularly unnerved by the bombing of what she called 'my bedroom.' After the Franklin County Sheriff's office and the Franklin County bomb squad had collected evidence and completed their preliminary investigation, Rachel approached Frank and asked to see the bedroom.

"I don't think that's a good idea," Frank said. "After all, it's not even your bedroom anymore. You're staying with Moselle and Barney."

"But I want to see it."

"You're an adult, Rachel, and you have the run of the property. I can't stop you, but I think it'll just freak you out. Why don't you talk to Barney about it?"

Rachel grimaced at Frank. She and Cane marched resolutely around the house to inspect the desolation of her old bedroom, still smoldering, and cordoned with yellow crime scene tape. She took several photographs with her phone and strode back to where Frank was standing. "Thank you for letting me see that. I could have been in there. I wouldn't be here anymore if I'd been in there."

"But you weren't there, and you *are* here," Frank said. "Try not to let what happened here last night change your life. If you can't do that, come to us and we'll arrange for you disappear, at least for a while. Helen can help you with that. Please think about it."

"I don't need to think about it. I want to disappear right now. This thing has gotten entirely out of hand. I want to start a new life somewhere else where nobody can find me. I want to be unknown."

"That's okay, too. We'll help you with that. The first thing you have to do is delete all the current photos and other material on your cell phone and on your computers. That's a clear giveaway of your previous whereabouts if somebody tries to find out about your past. We're also going to have to scrub your office—electronically and all the paperwork. You're going to really be starting over."

The creation of an alternate life for Rachel began at that moment. Helen flew in Jamie

Madden, her former associate--the masterful forger and grifter, to construct a new identity for Rachel. Jamie had many names, and he had credentials to support each one. He could do the same for anyone who had sufficient money to pay his fees. He prepared a new driver's license and passport along with other supporting documents for her. Rachel Brueggemann became Heidi Franklin with home and business addresses in Omaha. Frank funded a generous bank account for her, which supplemented her already large savings. All the money was wired to an Omaha bank under the name of Heidi Franklin. Heidi relocated to Omaha with her new identify and her dog, Cane, just in time for winter.

Tony had watched the air raid on the target house in St. Albans in real time through a video feed from the drone operators. He knew the layout of the house and was disappointed that Helen and Frank's bedroom had not been hit. He hated Helen with a vengeance and wanted to see her dead. When he thought about it, one out of two was pretty good, but he mentally underlined the elimination of Helen on his 'to do' list. The obliteration of the hacker's bedroom gave him some consolation. At least the woman who had exposed his financial duplicity was no longer in this world. He went to Mass early that Sunday morning, skipping confession. Tony felt certain he would sleep better that night.

After a long afternoon spent drinking Scotch and watching football on television, Tony dismissed his bodyguards at 10 p.m. An hour later he said, "Sam, you can go home early too. I haven't felt this good in days. I'm sure I can sleep tonight."

"Let me stay a little longer, sir, at least until you get to sleep. Then I'll slip out quietly. It's good to see you feeling better."

When Tony did not reply, Sam said, "I'll be in my office working on reports. I'll check on you before I leave."

Sam sat at his desk and texted the assassins that events were proceeding as planned. He busied himself moving papers around for a few minutes and then opened a pornography site on his computer. After about 10 minutes of watching pornography, he checked out cable news sites. Sam liked to look at several sites to stay informed politically. At midnight he looked in on Tony and found him sitting up in bed, staring at the opposite wall.

"I've just about finished, sir. Have you taken anything to help you sleep?"

Tony made a guttural sound and pointed to the empty pill vial on his bedside table.

"Good, sir, I'll just be a few more minutes. I'll check with you before I leave." Sam left the bedroom door ajar and returned to his office. He sat quietly reading the Chicago Tribune and waited until one a.m. He rose and checked Tony's bedroom to find him asleep, slumped sideways on several pillows. He returned to his office and gathered his papers. He texted the word 'proceed' to the assassins. He set the building alarms to activate at three a.m. — sufficient time for the killers to do their work and depart. He met them at the front door and let them in, before walking to his vehicle. Sam knew that he would need a few stiff drinks to sleep on this night.

The two killers carried only a small satchel. They took the elevator to Tony's sleeping area. In the outer room, they donned double gloves, masks, and full-face covers. They entered the bedroom and found Tony slumped over on his right side, snoring loudly. One took out the vial of carfentanil and with a medicine dropper, placed two drops in each nostril and another two drops in Tony's open mouth. He closed the bottle and they stood back. In about five minutes Tony's breathing became labored and then ceased. They waited another five minutes, and one stepped up and took his pulse. Tony was not breathing and had no pulse. The job was done. Not a sound had been made nor a word spoken.

They exited the building after placing their masks and face covers in the satchel. When the outer door closed behind them it was two a.m. "He'll sleep better tonight than he ever has," said one to the other.

"May he sleep with the devil," replied the other.

Tony's body was discovered by his daytime bodyguards at seven a.m. The body was cool but not yet stiff. The bodyguards notified Sam and Tony's other top associates and initiated a plan that Sam directed. A hearse from a funeral home picked up the body at 9 a.m. and transported it to an assistant coroner in a suburb, who certified Tony's cause of death to be a myocardial infarction. Paperwork was filed from the suburb for a death certificate. The body was cremated on the same day, and Tony's ashes were couriered back to his office building in River North. It was an apparently natural death in a city all too familiar with violent death.

જી

Vinnie Palermo discovered Tony had died when he read the brief obituary in the Chicago Tribune later that week. Tony was said to be a prominent Chicago businessman, who had died suddenly of a heart attack. Vinnie called Frank. "Tony Ragusa is dead," Vinnie said when Frank answered. "He died early Sunday morning. The obit says he died in his sleep."

"I don't believe it," Frank said. "Tony would be embarrassed to die so young and in his own bed. He would have much preferred a shootout or a bombing."

"I don't believe it either, Frank. I think it was a very sophisticated hit. But we'll never know. The body was cremated, and my source at the downtown medical examiner's office doesn't have any record of it. It was probably orchestrated out in the suburbs somewhere. I'm trying to get some information from a source I have in Tony's office, but so far I'm coming up empty. "

"You know I'm still sitting on his ten million from the SPAC fiasco, right?"

"Right … he wouldn't take it back. What do you think we should do?" Before Frank could consider an answer, Vinnie said, "Anyway, I need to talk to you about something else. Can you come up here? I'll send my plane."

"Vinnie, why can't we do this remotely?"

"It's family business. We need to discuss this in private."

"Then you can come down here. I want Helen to hear this anyway. She's the reason I'm babysitting the ten million."

Vinnie appeared at ten the next day, again squired by the same swarthy man, this time in an old Lincoln Town Car. He walked up to the house, kissed their cheeks, and accepted a glass of cold San Pellegrino Chinotto. Workers could be heard rebuilding the destroyed bedroom at one end of the house. They took seats at the other end on the terrace under the warm October sun. Vinnie opened his arms in an expansive way and said, "You two are living the life out here. Not a care in the world and rich as the devil himself."

"I wish it were so," said Frank. "We've become very unpopular around here since the drone attack. I think it's going to take a big investment in the village to buy back our respectability."

"I'm still very envious of you, but please let me get directly to the point. I'm in a financial bind. I've got loans coming due on real estate construction that I can't service. I don't want to lose my business."

"How much money do you need?"

"About twenty million in the next two months."

"I can help you, Vinnie, but I don't think your situation is going to get better any time soon."

Now it was Vinnie's turn to be silent. Helen sipped her mineral water and gazed at the distant river. Vinnie looked at Frank and forced a smile. "What do you think is going to happen, Frank?'

"Commercial real estate is dead for the immediate future. You've got to shift your financial direction to survive."

"What do you mean?"

"You've got to emphasize warehousing and fulfillment centers. Business is becoming all about the internet. People are staying home and ordering stuff off the internet. Business is being done remotely. Forget about building more traditional offices. Nobody's going there."

"Can you give me an outline... a business plan?" Vinnie was embarrassed to ask an old man this question. Especially an old man with no experience in commercial real estate. He loved his uncle, but he could see their roles of mentor and trainee reversing in a way that he had never imagined.

"Helen and I are essentially retired, and we're enjoying it. We're also trying to survive in this quaint little place after what recently happened up here at the house. We're being treated like we have the plague after last weekend…For your situation, I see a bare-bones plan looking something like this. You need to think warehousing and fulfillment centers. Let the big boys handle the logistics of moving stuff around. You build the bricks and mortar to house and sort stuff in the middle as it goes from supplier to wherever it ends up. You build it and lease it all back."

Vinnie was silent once more, visibly chastened. He knew he had again under-estimated his uncle. He also remembered that his accountants had been recommending a similar course of action.

"And here's another thing, Vinnie, since you're asking for advice, it's time to tighten your belt...change your lifestyle. The first thing is you don't need a plane. Think about the last time you used it. It was probably to fly down here over a month ago to talk about Tony and the SPAC deal. And you don't need a chauffeured limousine. Get a Ford or a Toyota and drive it yourself. Have your bodyguard ride shotgun if you think you still need that. Put some armor plate on it if you want... after all you live in downtown Chicago. It'll put a big dent in your gas mileage, but you'll probably feel a little safer."

"What about the ten million? I could sure use it right now."

"It's dirty money, Vinnie. Tony never made an honest buck in his life. We're going to marinate it."

"What the devil does that mean?"

"Move it around; put it through some heavy wash cycles and then wring it out a few times so that it looks old and clean. We're in the process of doing that now. It'll be marinated money."

"I need real money right now. I don't know anything about any of this marinated money."

"I'll have my bankers contact your people. We'll get your debts serviced with my clean assets, but you may have to restructure some of your loans. We'll have to see about that. Now let's have some lunch before you head back. We'll eat out here; you don't want to waste an October day in Missouri. We've still got a few fresh vegetables the rabbits didn't eat. I've made some spiedini, and we've got a nifty little Brunello to wash it down."

Helen joined Frank in bringing out the food and wine, and they dined on the terrace. They could see golfers below in the valley in one direction and towboats and barges making their way on the distant river to the west. Frank sensed that he had stung Vinnie with the lifestyle comments and tried to formulate some soothing chatter.

Before he could begin, Vinnie said, "This wine is really good, but the spiedini tastes a little different. It's good, mind you, just a little different."

"It's rabbit. Barney likes to hunt. He shoots them with a crossbow. He's the only reason we still have a few fresh vegetables around here," Frank said.

"He's your security guy, right? I know about him; is he looking for a job?"

"He's more than just security. He's about the smartest person I've ever known, but he's a free agent. You should talk to him if you want to hire him."

"Just asking. I've been getting some feelers from the East Coast people, and I may need to beef up my security. Nothing definite yet."

Helen, who had been pushing the spiedini around her plate, joined the conversation. "Vinnie, I'm surprised you didn't mention this before. If the East Coast people get involved in picking over the spoils of Tony's operation, it changes the whole equation for you and for us."

"It's all up in the air at this point, and I'm not sure Tony left much to pick over. I also understand they've moved Sam Mancuso into their Broward County operation. I don't know what's going to happen with Tony's outfit. As best I can tell it's a chaotic situation over on River North. They've cut off the head of the serpent, but the big snake's body is still thrashing."

They finished their lunch in silence, each one thinking about what the future might bring but reluctant to discuss it. After a polite interval, Vinnie thanked them and took his leave. Helen and Frank saw him off in the Lincoln Town Car, both wondering where he had obtained such an elegant old vehicle.

After the car descended from the bluff and turned a curve, Frank looked at Helen and said, "What happened to Tony is becoming clearer to me. Tony didn't die of a heart attack. If they've moved Sam Mancuso out, it means they killed Tony. They had inside help to do that, and that means Mancuso was involved."

"You know how those people think better than I do so you're probably right. What I think is that Vinnie is on the verge of joining them."

Chapter 11

Developments with the Covid-19 virus were mostly political in September of 2021. The president said in early September that he wanted to mandate vaccination for almost every adult. Scientists and physicians in government were offended that they had not been consulted, and several resigned in protest. The FDA and its outside advisory committee next made slightly different recommendations about vaccinations. Then the CDC and its advisory committee also made separate slightly different recommend-ations. These government agencies mostly based their recommendations on Israeli data that showed waning immunity with the Pfizer-BioNTech vaccine after about six months. The Israeli data ruled because the American CDC had been lax in collecting comparative data in the U.S. The individual states jealously tried to preserve their roles in this scrum, and the reality on the ground ranged from a free-for-all in Florida to get another shot, any shot, to a 'wait for the guidelines' approach elsewhere before offering the booster. All of this confused the public, but it only excited the media.

A large group of vaccine refusers continued to decline the shots, and some of them lost their jobs as a consequence. The surge in the delta variant appeared to be peaking at the end of September, which also encouraged vaccine refusals. Promising results with a pill to treat the infection emerged in early October. Molnupiravir from Merck was said to be available by the end of the year. A handful of these capsules taken twice daily for the first few days of infection appeared to cut the death rate and hospitalization rate in half. This development, while widely cheered, further encouraged those who opposed vaccination. Pfizer was also said to have an oral antiviral in their pipeline.

In Missouri, health systems began giving the Pfizer booster to elderly and other at-risk people the first week in October. Helen and Frank immediately took advantage of this and received the booster. Frank still was uncertain about Helen's actual age, but she had copious paperwork declaring her to be over sixty-five. Although Frank knew he could check her actual age on the internet, that idea did not seem conducive to domestic tranquility. He was happy for her to choose her age.

October weather in eastern Missouri continued to be ideal—warm and dry with occasional nocturnal rain showers. They ate on the terrace at lunch and supper. One day at lunch Frank said, "Vinnie called me today. The East Coast people want to have a sit-down with us."

"Us?"

"Vinnie and me. They want to talk about what's happening in Chicago."

"Why you? You're not in Chicago."

"I assume they're interested in our money. They like money."

"Darling, if you get involved with those people, you'll never be rid of them. It'll be worse than it was with Tony."

"I know. I told Vinnie that. He says he wants to meet with them. He wants me to sit in on it."

"May I sit in too?"

"Afraid not. They said no. They don't want you involved."

"Good Lord, a poor little old lady like me? How could I possibly be a threat to them?"

"My dear. They specifically said it was to be Vinnie and me. Nobody else."

"If you go to Chicago and leave me here, I can't promise I'll still be here when and if you come back. I think you're making a big mistake."

Frank did not reply. Helen sipped her San Pellegrino Limonata and toyed with a small plate of cold antipasto. Frank had finished eating and was enjoying a double espresso. They had hired a parttime chef to come in weekdays and prepare a hot lunch and leave a cold supper. Frank had decided he liked the chef, Andrea Simonetti, and tried not to be too critical of her cooking. He continued to cook on weekends when they entertained their small circle of friends. This arrangement gave Frank more time with his investment advisors and freed Helen from sous-chef duties. She could spend more time with Moselle at the country club. After the initial fear and condemnation had subsided, the drone attack had further increased Helen's cachet with prospective members. Everyone wanted to meet the woman who could hit a silver dollar at thirty feet and fight off killer drones with a shotgun. Helen's legend had far outgrown her reality.

Mozart's Piano Concerto No. 27 played softly in the front room. Frank finished his espresso and considered the complexities of wealth and leisure. Helen interrupted his ruminations. "I suppose you'll be flying over to New York or somewhere down in Florida." she said.

"No... they're coming here. I told them I'm not flying anywhere so they're all coming here on Saturday."

"Well, thanks for telling me! I hope you don't expect me to help entertain them. They don't even want to see me. I'll go down and have lunch at the club."

"Perfect. I think that's a wonderful idea. Andrea has agreed to come in Saturday morning and get some food ready for them. There'll only be two of them plus Vinnie and me. I don't think it will last long."

Vinnie called Frank the day before the meeting with the news that he was thinking about running Tony's waste management operation.

Frank was astonished. "What? Are you crazy? That's a den of thieves and thugs over on River North. You're asking for trouble."

"It will just be for a little while. I'm hoping you will come up here and get the ball rolling on our transition to remote work the way you laid it out to me. I really think you're the man to do that."

"Vinnie, are we both insane? I'm an old man. I'm retired, and I don't know my way around a commercial real estate operation. I don't know anything about it. I gave you the strategic picture. I can't do the tactical part of it."

"You don't have to. I've got people to do that. They'll handle the conversion of vacant properties to warehousing and fulfillment centers. They'll handle the construction and the robotics, seek out the contracts, and do the leases. You're family, Frank, *famiglia*. I need you"

"Then what would I do?"

You'd just oversee the big picture. Be sure they're going in the right direction…and hopefully you can light a fire under them the way you did me."

"I don't know, Vinnie. I'll have to think about it."

"You're going to hear about this tomorrow. I wanted to give you a heads up."

☙

Vinnie, Vito Ragusa, and Pasquale Salerno arrived at precisely ten a.m., squired by Vinnie's driver in the elegant old Town Car. Frank greeted them, and after the perfunctory exchange of kisses, led them out to the terrace. Andrea had already laid out some antipasto and drinks on a side table before she departed. They sat around a large round table shaded by a wide umbrella. After sampling the antipasto, Patsy finally began, "Thank you again for inviting us, Frank. You have a beautiful place out here. We've come to put a proposal in front of you. We hope you will give it close consideration."

Frank looked solemn, and Vinnie forced a smile. Patsy continued, "As you know Tony Ragusa's operation is in disarray, may he rest in peace. Vinnie here has agreed to be the acting boss of the waste management operation until we can establish some order and put in some leadership out here."

Frank tried to be nonchalant. "What do you want from me?" he asked.

Vinnie spoke up. "We want you to be the temporary head of my commercial real estate operation. Everybody likes your ideas about transitioning to more remote work situations."

"Vinnie, I have to say I'm flattered and surprised, but you must have people in your office who can do this. I'm an old man, and I'm not familiar with your day-to-day operation. I want to help, but I can only give you a few weeks. Then you'll need a younger guy to do this. I'll just help him get started."

Frank found himself getting angry at the way these men made assumptions about him. He looked at Vito and said, "You two are acting bosses in New York and South Florida, right? Nobody's a real boss these days. You guys are as disorganized as Tony. You don't have an organization anymore. You're beginning to sound like the federal government. You'd be better off going out and buying some lottery tickets than trying to run Tony's operation."

"Nobody talks to me like that, especially an old man like you," Patsy said.

Frank swallowed and summoned more courage. "Well, Patsy, you're at least as old as I am, and I'm talking to you like that right now. If you can't be moral, at least be competent. You've got no succession plan; you're not tech savvy and you don't understand modern finance. You have no women in your organization. You're missing half the brainpower that's out there. You're living in the last century. You still settle everything with guns and bombs."

Vito and Patsy looked at each other in feigned disbelief. Vinnie managed a faint smile. Finally, Patsy said, "You make a point. Frank. I'll admit we've lost some ground recently, and we're getting old. Nobody can deny that. But we're going to change."

"What are you going to do—go to Harvard Business School and learn spreadsheets?"

"Your family always had the smart mouth, and I see that hasn't changed. I'm willing to overlook your disrespect because we know there's money in what Tony was doing. He was crazy as a loon at the end, but he was still making money. We already have something like it on the East Coast, and we think we can make the Chicago operation run right. Help us and we'll help you."

"How can you help us?" Vinnie said.

"We can give you access to our political contacts and to some financial assets. The feds were about to come down hard on Tony's operation. We can help with that."

"You can make the feds take the heat off Tony?" Vinnie asked.

"Yes, we can help with that," Vito said.

"We'll give you a month, and it's going to cost you. I'll have my accountants send you the numbers."

Frank winced; he had only promised them two weeks. He was beginning to feel the effect of a strong undertow pulling him into deep water, but he kept silent.

The meeting with the temporary and acting East Coast bosses ended on that note—a cold truce. Vinnie's driver squired Vito and Patsy back to the airport, and Vinnie said he would stay a little longer to iron out the details of Frank's role. When Vito and Patsy had gone, Frank said, "Vinnie, I can't believe you're doing this."

"You don't understand. They've got leverage on me. They're saying they killed my parents."

"I thought your parents died in a car accident outside Naples."

They're saying their people forced the car off that steep road. It was not an accident. They're saying they'll forget about the problems my father caused them when he was a prosecutor if I help them now. I don't have a choice."

"Of course, you do; you have a clear choice. You can walk away from them. If your parents were murdered, you have no idea who did it. In Naples, it could have been any number of people."

"It'll just be for a little while until I can get Tony's operation organized and restructured. They want to move in on waste management. They say it's the future in the Midwest and they want a piece of it out here. They want to make it work like they're trying to do on the East Coast."

"Once they get their hooks into you, you're theirs for life. You must know this is the way they operate. You can walk away now. I'll help you. Please listen to me."

"Frank, right now the only thing I need is for you to run the commercial real estate transition. You can do it from ten thousand feet. Just give me some time. I'm trying to sort this thing out. I told them they need to spin off the street operation. I'm talking about the shakedowns and extortion. I want that operation completely out of the River North complex; I don't want any part of that. They've agreed to send a guy out from New York to run that part of the business. They'll do it out of Tony's show office just off Michigan Avenue."

Frank relented against his better judgment. "Michigan Avenue sounds like a better place than most for extortion and shakedowns, but I don't think they can get away with it, even in Chicago. Please hear me, Vinnie. I'm telling you what I told them. I will give you two weeks. I'll go up to Chicago and get things rolling on the transition in your real estate business. After that, you're on your own if you keep playing ball with them."

Chapter 12

By the middle of October, it became apparent to almost everyone, even several high government officials, that the economy was slowing down and that supply chains were in danger of gridlock. Small businesses were closing for lack of employees. The price of food, gasoline, and everything else was going up. In California, multiple ships remained anchored off the ports of Long Beach and Los Angeles because they could not be unloaded, and trucks were in short supply to distribute the unloaded goods. One huge container ship apparently dragged its anchor across an underwater pipeline—resulting in a large oil spill—and fires broke out in shipping containers ashore. These events spurred some activity in the California ports, but the backlog would take weeks to remedy. Union Pacific announced that it would run trains day and night to help with the congestion. Officials warned that Christmas might lack presents. The public was becoming restive, and politicians found themselves in even greater disfavor.

In Chicago, amidst this societal upheaval, Vinnie tried to root out the ingrained criminal mentality of Tony's people, and Frank tried to shift Vinnie's people from the mindset of traditional commercial real estate to on-line working, which meant operating warehouses and fulfillment centers instead of office buildings. Of their two tasks, Vinnie recognized that his would be more difficult—he not only had to restructure and refinance Tony's legitimate waste management operation, but he had to rehabilitate and refocus a motley group of thugs and brigands. He moved several of them over to the spin-off street crime operation near Michigan Avenue. The few who remained were incorrigible and untrainable and would have to be let go. Firing these people made Vinnie anxious because their responses would be unpredictable … they were armed and just smart enough to see their immediate future.

He called Frank and made further inquiries about Barney's availability. "I've found I really need somebody like Barney," he said. "Most of these guys around here are packing, and all of them are pissed off."

"Barney's a free agent. You'll have to make your pitch to him."

"He won't budge. He likes it too much working for you … and his wife is afraid to move up here."

"You've obviously already talked to him. And Moselle is spot on to be afraid of Chicago."

"Well … actually, I did. He refused me, but he helped me find a buddy of his here in Chicago to help with security. He's a big guy like Barney, and he's looking at a job with us. I think he'll scare the appropriate people around this place."

By the first week of November, new cases and deaths from the pandemic continued to ebb, but inflation, supply bottlenecks and political ineptitude increased. Elections on November 2nd signaled voter dissatisfaction with the performance of politicians far and wide. Parents were unhappy with the public education system. The initial fatigue among the population had shifted to unease. People were acting and voting accordingly.

ↄ

Frank remained in Chicago longer than he had intended, staying in Vinnie's spare bedroom, and overseeing the shift in Vinnie's business. He called Helen several times, but she would not pick up or return his calls. He tried texting her, but she did not respond to his texts. Finally, she answered his call late one Friday afternoon in early November. "Thanks for answering," Frank said. "I just wanted to tell you I miss you."

"I miss you too."

"Where are you?"

"I'm home."

"Home as in up on the bluff."

"It's the only home I have. I'm looking at the river right now. It's beautiful ... shining like silver and gold in the setting sun. The trees are turning red and yellow. You should see it."

"That's good. Things are going pretty well up here. I should be home by Thanksgiving week. Vinnie's people have made the transition relatively easy. They're good at following orders… not so good at independent thinking."

"I'm sure you've helped them with the thinking part. While you've been working or whatever it is you're doing up there, I've been thinking too. May I ask where the marinated money is now?"

"It's pretty much fully marinated at this point. It was dirty money, but it's been scrubbed so much, it almost looks clean. I've got it parked in a charitable foundation I set up in Delaware."

"Good. My ideas about what to do with it are coming into focus."

"I've been thinking about it too. Please tell me your ideas."

"I think you should choose a good cause, and I'll choose one. Then we'll give the money to those causes and credit Vito and Patsy. I'm sure you can figure out the details of how to make this work."

"I like that. We should give Tony some credit in this charity deal too. The three of them — the great philanthropists — that makes me smile. Then we shower them with publicity. They'll love it, and it'll throw them so far off their game, they'll forget the score … at least for a while."

"What's your cause?" Helen asked.

"I would give half to the St. Vincent Home here in St. Louis. They do good work with children before it's too late to save them. I served on their board back when I was running the restaurant, and I was impressed with what they do."

"I like your idea," Helen said. "I think we should give the other half to Barney to help buy back the Benin Bronzes. He can use it to help purchase the bronzes from private collectors in North America. It looks like the museums are already falling in line and will return their collections."

"That's sounds like a good cause," Frank said.

"You'd better clear this with Vinnie. We both know he doesn't like to give away money."

Frank ran their charitable ideas by a reluctant Vinnie, who still considered the ten million to be his money. Frank emphasized the benefits of positive publicity for the East Coast crowd and Tony's memory, telling Vinnie it might soften the avaricious ways of Vito and Patsy. Vinnie was not happy. "Oscar Wilde said the only bad publicity is no publicity. We don't need to buy publicity for those people; I say we keep the money and forget about them."

"Vinnie, I didn't know you were familiar with Oscar Wilde."

"He's like the rest of us. He was always needing money ... and publicity."

"You'll get plenty of publicity from this, my dear nephew. The money's coming from a foundation I set up for you to distribute money to our East Coast friends. Helen and I designed it so anybody with average intelligence and a little effort can trace the money from you to the other three, living and dead. You're going to look very good... and they're going to look even better."

Half of the thoroughly marinated money moved from the charitable foundation to an established 501c3 fund to help recover the remaining Benin Bronzes in North America and return them to Nigeria. Barney was named as the administrator. The other half went to the St. Vincent Home in St. Louis—a small residential school for troubled youth and their families. Helen and Frank had their bank prepare press releases about the putative donors---the East Coast Italian Social Club and the Anthony Ragusa Memorial Fund. Media sleuths could identify the first outfit because it actually existed, but the second was more difficult to trace.

Vito and Patsy were specifically named as the principal donors from the social club. They were widely known in New York and South Florida from previous indictments and court appearances. Neither of them had ever been convicted of a crime or done prison time, but stories of their criminal predilections continued to swirl around them. As the publicity bubble enlarged, none of this seemed to matter; the money was real, and it was going to good causes.

Patsy and Vito became famous, at least in parts of South Florida and New York City. The unsavory backgrounds of these two elderly mobsters thoroughly piqued public interest when the charitable awards were announced. Both men had never been recognized as supporters of charity. The public was surprised, then amazed, and ultimately gratified by such unexpected altruism.

Patsy and Vito were initially puzzled and suspicious about the charitable largess that was attributed to them, and they had never heard of the St. Vincent Home or the Benin Bronzes. They ordered their accountants and computer experts to find the source of the money and get information on the two recipients of their charity. When identifying the source of the money proved difficult and with their public approval soaring, the two acting bosses rose to the occasion and basked in the glory of being big charitable donors.

Vito was quoted in New York newspapers as always wanting to help troubled children in St. Louis and people in Africa who had been wronged. He was simply happy to finally be given the opportunity to make this happen with his two substantial donations. Patsy was interviewed on a Fort Lauderdale television station and expressed similar long-standing if previously unrecognized charitable sentiments. Tony, of course, could not speak for himself, and little information could be unearthed about the Anthony Ragusa Memorial Fund. This fund seemed to have materialized in service of the two charitable donations and thereafter disappeared. Tony Ragusa became much more admirable in death than he had ever been in life.

In the real world, the East Coast operatives slowly took control of Tony's waste management business after Vinnie had stabilized its financial situation, an improvement for which Vinnie received a substantial payment. Vinnie still owned his commercial real estate firm, and Frank continued to help him with the transition to support remote work. These operational changes would be largely in place by the end of November although the ultimate profitability of Tony's waste disposal operation continued in doubt. Tony's street operation of shakedowns and extortion remained a festering sore. Vito and Patsy decided to downgrade and ultimately liquidate that part of Tony's business. It was becoming a lug on their charitable reputations and legitimate business aspirations.

Frank returned home the Tuesday before Thanksgiving to a joyous welcome from Helen, who had decided she really missed him. Vinnie would join them the next day, and they planned to dine Thursday with a festive, unmasked and appropriately distanced crowd at a lavish afternoon dinner at the country club. There were many illustrious members of this club, and the notoriety of Helen, Frank and Vinnie no longer aroused any particular curiosity. It only added to the celebration. The three surviving members of this branch of the Palermo family had much to be thankful for—their very lives, their retained wealth, and their health. As an added bonus, the pandemic seemed to be ebbing although the uncertainty of winter loomed ominously, and some locales were reporting increases in Covid infections.

Barney and Moselle had traveled to Georgia and were enjoying their holiday with extended family. Vinnie's entire crew in Chicago had been given the long weekend off. In additional signs of the times, Vinnie had leased his plane indefinitely and given his driver the weekend off. He had flown coach to St. Louis and reserved a rental Ford sedan in St. Louis. When he arrived, the only vehicle remaining in the lot was a Ford F-150 pickup truck. Still wearing his suit and tie, he drove the truck out to meet Frank and Helen atop the bluff in St. Albans.

"I like your ride, Vinnie," Frank said when Vinnie pulled up. "But it looks like you forgot your boots and cowboy hat."

It was the only vehicle left when I got to the rental lot so go easy on the sarcasm. I gave my driver the weekend off, and my old Town Car is being repaired. That car is way past its prime for a long road trip. I flew down and wound up with this monster."

"Frank can loan you some jeans and a cowboy shirt. You'll fit in perfectly around here with the good old boys in Lincoln County," Helen said.

"How's Rachel doing?" Vinnie asked. "I've been looking forward to seeing her while I'm down here."

"Rachel is out of touch right now," Frank said.

"What does 'out of touch' mean? She's doing okay, I hope. There's nothing wrong with her, right? I really liked her in the video."

"She fine. She just can't be reached right now."

Vinnie realized the subject of Rachel was closed to further conversation. He took his overnight bag into the house, unpacked, and changed into casual clothing, making a mental note to check out Rachel's whereabouts through his other sources.

Thursday delivered an overcast and briskly cool day, sufficiently pleasant for late November that they had driven down to the club in Frank's golf cart for the afternoon feast.

After they were seated and served, Vinnie raised a glass of prosecco and proposed a dubious toast. "Here's to the ten million we lost, and here's to what we gained, although I still wonder what it is."

"We bought protection with that money," Frank said. "We greased the skids to get us out from under the East Coast crowd. I really would prefer to live my life without those guys around. Painting them as big-time philanthropists helped us do that."

"I'm not so sure about that, darling," Helen said. "They seem to be more around you now than they were before. They have control of Tony's waste management operation. Given their business skills and previous performance, they'll find a way to screw that up. Then they'll come after Vinnie's commercial real estate business too. Mark my words."

"Well, at least it buys us some time. When they come back for Vinnie's part, we'll sell them the commercial real estate operation at a premium, and Vinnie will keep the warehouses and fulfillment centers for remote work. I think it will make everybody happy, at least from the financial point of view, although I'm not sure if Vito and Patsy are ever really happy. Can you live with that plan, Vinnie?"

Vinnie frowned. "I didn't come down here to talk business with you two. Let's just enjoy the present. We'll cross that bridge when we come to it."

"That won't be long," Helen said.

Frank grinned, and they again clinked glasses. "That sounds like another plan ... and a prediction. Let's enjoy our holiday bird and have a glass or two of this shy little Barbaresco I brought over from the house. This turkey here is as good as I could have made myself, moist and tasty. It's a fine day to celebrate and be happy together. We'll worry about tomorrow when it comes."

"The cliches are cutting a wide swath through here," Helen said and sipped her wine. "You gentlemen make a good team. You think alike; you talk alike. I think you should continue to work together."

"I agree with that. What do you plan to do, Frank?"

"In the immortal words of Yogi Berra, 'It's tough to make predictions, especially about the future.' Right now, I'm thinking I'm going to enjoy the next month around here and then head down to my lake house in Florida for January and February. I'll catch some fish and enjoy the warm weather. What about you, Vinnie?"

"I'm going to try to keep my head above water with my new business direction. Frank here, my esteemed uncle, has me mortgaged to the hilt again."

"And Helen, what about you?" Vinnie asked with trepidation.

"I plan to try to keep you two out of trouble," Helen said. "You also need someone to help you with public relations … supply you with better talking points. You both tend to go way too heavy on the aphorisms."

I sincerely hope you enjoyed this second Helen and Frank story. Please add a short review online where you purchased your copy and let me know your thoughts!

Turn the page for a sneak peek
of

Russians and Rubles

A Helen and Frank Story

Chapter 1

December of 2021 brought no relief from Covid-19. The Omicron mutation of the virus, which had appeared around Thanksgiving, was highly infectious. It spread quickly, and efforts to contain it proved futile. Authorities argued about masks, vaccines, testing, isolation, and public gatherings. The one subject they dared not discuss was another lockdown. Various agencies issued conflicting guidelines and recommendations. When vaccinations were mandated for many private employees, the public was appalled by seeing healthcare workers, who had labored so hard and risked so much earlier in the pandemic, lose their jobs for refusing the vaccine. The irony was compounded when authorities recognized their mistake and issued exemptions to get essential people back to work. Even the definition of 'essential' was intensely debated. Test kits to detect infection were in short supply as were monoclonal antibodies to treat severe infections. Media personalities and pundits ignored the evidence that Omicron infection usually resulted in mild illness and that this variant might signal transition of the virus from pandemic to endemic status. The growing number of infected people disrupted travel and holiday activities. Health officials warned that hospitals could be overwhelmed. Rates of violent crime, suicide, drug overdoses and traffic fatalities increased. Despite this turmoil, people seemed determined to get on with their lives and mostly ignored everything that didn't affect their immediate needs.

At home in St. Albans, Missouri, on New Year's Eve, Francis Cabrini Palermo showered quickly and shivered as he toweled off. His bathroom was warm but the frigid cold outside seemed to permeate the entire house. He put on shorts and socks and inspected himself in the dressing room mirror. His fallen chest and protuberant belly were disappointing. He leaned forward for a closer inspection of his face and found it sagging too. Wrinkles and skin folds were winning everywhere he looked; his chest and legs seemed to be migrating to his stomach and hips. Even taking a deep breath and sucking in his abdomen failed to help. Frank thought he was beginning to look like a pear standing on toothpicks. He sighed as he exhaled. Based on what he saw, the year 2022 did not look promising for his body. Frank hoped his mind would hold up better. He pulled out his tuxedo and made a new year's resolution to get rid of the full-length mirror in his dressing room.

Helen came to the door and smiled. She looked beautiful in her little black dress and diamond stud earrings — ready for cocktails with Barney and Moselle and the party to follow at the country club.

"Admiring ourselves in the mirror again, are we?"

Frank, still in socks and shorts, turned and tried to return her smile.

"Not much left anymore to admire. I think I'll get rid of the mirror … don't like what it's showing me."

"That's why I don't have any full-length mirrors in my dressing room. I concentrate on my face. I can cover up the rest."

"Every part of you looks great." Frank was careful to omit the word 'still' from his attempt to praise her. "I'll be with you in a minute."

"Don't hurry, and you won't have to tussle with the tuxedo. The club has cancelled the party," she said.

"Oh, no. What's going on?"

"Several members of the band called in sick this afternoon, and the wait staff is short-handed because of Covid. The general manager texted his apologies for such short notice, but they simply can't pull it off. Covid is turning everything upside down again."

"I'm not surprised, my dear. I was beginning to wonder if any of the members would show up. Everybody's afraid of Covid again because of this variant. This virus is the curse that keeps on cursing, but we can still go have drinks with Barney and Moselle. We'll play some music and party with them."

"Afraid not, darling. Moselle just texted me too. She thinks she's coming down with something. She's afraid it might be Omicron, and she's been vaccinated."

"Can Barney come up here? I can ice a bottle of Champagne, and there's Prosecco in the wine cooler."

"Negative on that too. They're both self-isolating… they don't want to spread anything until they know what's happening. I don't blame them. I think we should self-isolate too. We've been around them a lot in the last few days. It looks like we're on our own tonight."

Helen and Frank's New Year's Eve of 2021 had begun with big plans, but it ended with a half-bottle of Prosecco and the rerun of a musical program on PBS. They were in bed by eleven p.m. with the shared hope that 2022 would be a better year.

New Year's Day dawned cold and cloudy. The distant Missouri River far below them looked like a giant gray snake. They had lox and bagels with the usual trimmings and finished the Prosecco, which had gone flat. Vincenzo Alessandro Palermo, Frank's nephew, called at eleven a.m. from Chicago. Frank put him on speaker phone.

"Happy New Year, you two. I'm guessing you partied all night and are just waking up."

"Our entire evening crashed and burned. Covid won again. We stayed home and watched television," Frank said.

"Same here. Chicago is trying to lock down again… at least that's what the schoolteachers are saying. I think we'll be working from home for a while in the waste management operation … except for the collection teams. They'll be out there making a few pick-ups, but that'll be it."

Frank paused. He knew Vinnie wanted something from them but was having trouble getting to the point. "How's business, Vinnie? I imagine the East Coast people are pretty much running waste management by now."

"Right. I'm almost back fulltime with the commercial real estate business and the transition plans you put in." Vinnie took a deep breath. "Say… Frank. I've been trying to find Rachel Bruggemann, but I'm coming up empty. Can you help me?"

Helen jumped in. "Vinnie, I think you're interested in her. You want to date her; am I right?"

Vinnie hesitated again. "She's very attractive … and smart. I'd like to get to know her better."

Now Frank hesitated. "Here's the deal, Vinnie. Rachel got very anxious about Tony Ragusa and the SPAC deal that went bad, and I think she was right to be anxious. We were dealing with some very unsavory people at the time. She requested that we arrange for her to disappear… at least for a while, and we helped her. I'm glad you're having trouble finding her."

"I understand. Maybe you could contact her… see if she wants to talk to me. It wouldn't be about business. It would be a purely social contact."

"Vinnie, I'll talk to her, but I think this is a bad idea. If you start seeing her, your colleagues in New York and South Florida are bound to find out, and Vito and Patsy may think they still have a score to settle with her."

Helen nodded in silent agreement.

"They're not my colleagues! I keep them at arms-length. They're pretty much running waste management up here now after I helped them get started. I'm just barely involved with them anymore. I kept my end of the bargain. Now I want to be done with the whole lot of them."

Frank was not convinced. "Alright, Vinnie, I'll contact her and see if she wants to hear from you. Please stop trying to find her while I do this. I'll get back to you, okay?"

When Frank put down the phone, Helen said, "I think you'd be making a big mistake if you pull Rachel back into this. She could get hurt."

"I want to have some control if they start seeing each other. If I don't contact her, he'll find her anyway. You remember how he always found us when we tried to hide. And I'll bet his East

Coast friends will find her through him."

"You'd better warn her about this."

"She's all grown up. She knows about Vinnie and those people. She can make her own decisions, but I'd like to know what she's doing. I almost feel like she's our daughter."

Helen looked at Frank and shook her head in disbelief. He left an encrypted message for Rachel through a confidential server. He told her that Vinnie wanted to see her socially and asked her to get back to him with her decision. When he didn't get a response for several days, he began making plans to drive to Florida where he would stay at his lakefront cabin for two months. Helen had decided not to accompany him. She told him the little cabin in Interlachen was too rustic for her. She did insist that Barney accompany him on the trip down and then fly back from Jacksonville. Frank was packing when he began to notice a headache and sore throat. Then fever set in, and every part of his body began to ache. He took an Advil that gave little relief. By the next day, the malady had spread into his chest with congestion and a cough.

The day before he was scheduled to leave, Helen said, "I've seen you popping my Advil. Are you okay?"

"I think it's just a little head cold, but it seems to be getting into my chest and the rest of my body."

"You probably have Omicron. I have a home test kit. Let's check you out."

Frank reluctantly agreed. He had never been fond of doctors and nurses, particularly when they began ordering tests and telling him what to do. He had also heard that the rapid antigen tests were little better than a coin-flip for Omicron. When the test registered negative, he felt relief and returned to packing. He and Barney would make the drive to Florida over two days. Frank would drop him off at the Jacksonville airport for his return flight before continuing to his lakefront cabin in Interlachen. He could already feel the warm sunshine. He had fond memories of the solitude of the little cabin on beautiful Lake Susan.

The next morning, Helen said, "You don't look so good. You're pale. You look like what my mother used to call peaked. I have another test kit. Let's check you again. I hear sometimes the tests can be negative before they turn positive."

When the second test returned positive, Frank felt despondent, and Helen was vindicated.

"See, I told you. You've got Covid. You need to call your doctor and get some medicine. Now you'll give it to me too."

"I think you gave it to me. You're the one who's always going down to the club and having lunch with Moselle. I stay up here on the bluff and don't see anybody. And I'm not calling my doctor. I'm just not that sick, and I know she'll say to stay home and do exactly what I'm doing."

"Whatever you say, Dr. Palermo. Anyway, I'm sleeping in the far bedroom and staying away from *you*."

Frank did call his doctor, who told him to stay home and keep taking Advil or Tylenol if he felt feverish. She also suggested he use an inhaled steroid for the cough. She called in a prescription for a budesonide inhaler, which he did not fill when he learned the cost. After several days of extreme fatigue and cough, he slowly began to regain some stamina. The cough lingered. He resisted any additional medication and by the third week of January felt sufficiently improved to depart for Florida. Helen said no to this idea, insisting that he remain at home for another week. She communicated this decision by cellphone from the other end of the house.

When Helen thought he was no longer infectious, she returned to his end of the house and began to ply him with canned chicken soup, vitamins, minerals, and several herb mixtures. After three days of her ministrations, Frank was determined to depart no matter what his condition. He put his investments on hold, packed his car, picked up Barney, and they left for Florida on the first day of February.

♔♔♔

The trip to Florida was uneventful. Barney insisted on accompanying Frank to the lake cabin and helped him move in, which was fortuitous because the cabin and the rowboat needed some minor repairs. After a week when they had set everything to rights, Frank drove Barney to the Jacksonville airport for his return trip to St. Louis. Frank returned to the little cabin on Lake Susan and prepared for two months of peace and quiet. Helen had dispatched him to Florida with a supply of vitamins, minerals, and herbs. She texted him daily to be sure he was taking care of himself, which meant that he was doing what she had instructed. Frank quickly found that he preferred the isolated cabin a year ago when he and Helen were hiding from Tony and had shut down all communication to the outside world. He texted Helen that he was trying to recapture that time by turning off his cellphone.

The Florida sunshine worked its magic. As Frank felt his strength return, the cough subsided. He had never lost his sense of taste or smell. By the middle of February, he was out in the rowboat daily, trying to outwit the fish, which seemed to have gotten smarter since last year. His solitude helped him realize that he missed Helen's wit and snappy repartee. He began having erotic dreams about her — dreams he had long ago decided he would never have again. Out in his boat, he could smell the sweet scent from early blooming grapefruit trees around the lake. He imagined he could smell Helen and feel her touch. She had become integral to his life. He decided he would only stay one month in Florida. If she would not come to him, he would have to go to her.

He turned on his cellphone the last week in February to inform Helen of his decision and found a text message from Rachel. She simply wrote, 'Thank you for getting me together with Vinnie. We've had two dates. I think he's fabulous.' There were two heart emojis at the beginning and end of the message. Helen had also texted him that Vinnie had found Rachel and was dating her. The remainder of his text messages were requests for donations.

Migratory waterfowl landing on the lake and departing on their way north cemented Frank's decision. He decided he would return to St. Louis at the end of February. If Rachel's new relationship with Vinnie became public knowledge, he wanted to try to exert some control. He texted Helen, shut down the cabin, drove to the Jacksonville airport and took a Southwest flight to St. Louis.

Helen met him at Lambert Airport. They kissed and walked directly to her Uber. Frank had only a small carry-on bag. His Florida clothing would be useless in St. Louis weather in March.

"I'm glad to see you," he said. "I really missed you. The little cabin felt empty without you."

"You really came back to see about Rachel, didn't you?"

"I came back to see you, but I'm worried about her. I guess Vinnie found her. I was surprised at how quickly they got together."

"Prepare to be more surprised," she said. "They're in Vegas as we speak. I think they're getting married."

About the Author

Thomas Morgan is Thomas Morgan Hyers, a practicing pulmonologist in St. Louis. He is in the same age group as the two principal characters in the Helen and Frank stories, and he continues to experience the pandemic years of Covid-19 in his medical practice and in his personal interactions with family and friends. This is his second book in the series, in which he weaves the effect of the pandemic on the lives of his fictional characters. He practices pulmonary occupational medicine and conducts clinical research with new pharmaceuticals. In addition to his medical responsibilities and writing efforts, he likes to spend time with his family, garden and cook.

www.ingramcontent.com/pod-product-compliance
Lightning Source LLC
Chambersburg PA
CBHW070354200726
48294CB00003B/897